History in Things

M.T.W. Cruise

M.T.W. Cruise Books

History in Things

History in Things

M.T.W. Cruise

M.T.W. Cruise Books

M.T.W. Cruise Books: P.O. Box 208, Dublin, VA 24084

Publisher's Note
This is a work of fiction. Names, characters, places, and incidents either are the product of the author's imagination or are used fictitiously, and any resemblance to actual persons, living or dead, business establishments, events, or locales is entirely coincidental.

Cover Design by Melanje'

Library of Congress Control Number: 2014905897

ISBN - 13: 978-0-9790433-4-5
ISBN - 10: 0-9790433-4-4

Printed in the United States of America

Mom,
You were always in my corner, always cheering me
on. "I see you." I love you eternally.

For Uncle Bob
a.ka.
"Uncle Ned"
Our family <u>guewel</u> - historian and master
storyteller.

History in Things

Preface

The contents of the following story includes the central character's retrospection on the importance of continuity in family history, both conversely and adversely. The terms Colored, Negro, Black, and African American are used synonymously, depicting the term of the time. Quotations introducing various chapters reflect spirituals and writings pertinent to the culture and nature of the times as African Americans progressed from the bonds of slavery to their present day status.

M.T.W. Cruise

"...and if a race has no history, if it has no worth-while tradition, it becomes a negligible factor in the thought of the world, and it stands in danger of extermination."

Carter G. Woodson, 1926

I

1
All Blues

It hadn't happened all at once, but gradually. Melancholy had grown slowly, its roots deep. An irrepressible dread came over Lemuel every time he walked through his office door.

The dreams had begun again, too; a recurring dream that had begun in college. In it, he repeatedly forgot to attend the history class in which he was enrolled. He would awake relieved to find it had only been a dream, but it always left him with the unsettling feeling that he'd forgotten to do something or rather that time was running out.

Sitting at his desk, he turns over and over in his hand the unopened letter left him by his great-aunt upon her recent death.

Aunt "T" had never had any children of her own. Being the oldest, she helped to rear her two younger siblings after the untimely deaths of their parents.

She, too, knew what it meant to be orphaned at an early age. This fact had made her and Lemuel kindred spirits of sorts.

M.T.W. Cruise

Vashti "T" relocated from Richmond to Washington, D.C., to live with her sister's family after the death of her beloved husband of over fifty years. Having never had any children of their own they had, in later years, affectionately referred to each other as "Mother" and "Daddy." Their hand at helping to rear countless nieces and nephews had certainly earned them that right.

Vashti remained in the family home after the deaths of her sister and brother-in-law. She had kept it up as best she could until she, too, had succumbed to the effects of old age. She died at the unbelievable age of 101.

Lemuel had been at her bedside when she'd passed away. It had conjured up memories of his grandmother's death. Alzheimer's had seemed to rob her of her very soul. When he looked into her eyes there was a vacancy where his grandmother's soul had once thrived.

He remembered viewing her body at the funeral. To his surprise, in the coffin lay the face of the spirited and vibrant grandmother he remembered. It was as if her spirit had been temporarily restored upon her death.

Aunt "T's" death had in no way resembled that of his grandmother. Her body had failed her in the end but her mind had been as sharp as ever. Her death had brought to his mind the James

Weldon Johnson poem *Go Down Death*.   She hadn't been afraid of death but rather welcomed it. In the end, she had simply smiled as if greeting an old friend and closed her eyes peacefully.

Death both fascinated and frightened him.   He remembered, vividly, as a child listening to his father and grandfather speak of his great-grandmother's passing.   In those days the mortician would come to the house with a portable embalming kit and prepare the body for viewing right in the home where the body would remain until the funeral.   At the time, Lemuel couldn't imagine sleeping in the same house with a dead body, even if it **was** a loved one.

Looking up at the framed autographed Phylliss Hyman t-shirt, a wedding anniversary gift from his wife, Lemuel reminisces about the night they'd first met.

Home one weekend from Hampton University during his junior year, he had gone, begrudgingly, on a double date with his best friend to Blues Alley. His date had been attractive and pleasant enough but there was no spark.

A stately Phyllis Hyman had come into the club's entrance a few minutes before show time. Looking absolutely regal in one of her signature hats, she had come over to their table and greeted them before taking the stage.

Asia, their cocktail waitress, had taken them up to Ms. Hyman's dressing room to have the t-shirts they'd purchased autographed after the show. Slyly, she had slipped him a cocktail napkin on which she had written her name and dorm number as they were leaving.

Asia was a sophomore at Howard University in the pre-med program with aspirations of becoming a veterinarian. Lemuel was back and forth from Hampton to D.C. just about every weekend after that, much to the delight of his grandmother. By the end of his senior year, he knew he was going to ask her to marry him.

After graduating from Hampton, Lemuel was accepted into Howard's Dental School, his grandfather's alma mater.

Upon graduating from Howard, Asia was accepted into the University of Maryland's veterinary program.

Now, all these years later they were, by all outward accounts, living the American dream. They had two beautiful and well-adjusted kids, an upscale home in Ft. Washington, Maryland, drove expensive cars, and could afford to pamper themselves with exotic vacations.

M.T.W. Cruise

Admittedly, it was his wife's veterinary practice that afforded them most of what they had. This wasn't the source of his anguish. On the contrary, he was proud of Asia and envied her the fact that she had followed her passion and was able to thrive doing it. He didn't have the passion for the dental profession that he'd once had.

Few people have medical insurance for their pets. Veterinarians don't have to hassle with insurance companies for adequate compensation. It's still a mostly cash-for-services rendered business. Nor do veterinarians have to bother with malpractice insurance because, while most pets are treated like members of the family, legally they are considered property. Veterinarians can't be sued for more than the face value of a pet.

In many respects, the veterinary practice is no different than the human practice of medicine before insurance companies dictated policy and the increasing threat of lawsuits guided medical decisions.

It never ceases to amaze Lemuel that while the majority of Americans can't afford medical insurance for themselves and their children, the veterinary business continues to thrive. Today, solo medical and dental practices fight to keep their heads above water to pay staff salaries, ever-increasing business overhead, and skyrocketing malpractice insurance.

Health insurance bureaucracy and micromanagement have distracted physicians from focusing on patient care and has all but driven the majority of solo primary care physicians and dentists out of business.

During his grandfather's day, Negro doctors and dentists were held in the highest regard. It wasn't about money, it was about giving back to the community. It was caring about people and filling a void in the Negro community that white society, in many cases, was unwilling to provide. It was educating the community about health and hygiene. It was giving the Negro community someone to look up to and something for which to aspire.

Turning the envelope over one last time, Lemuel opens it:

August 27, 2008

Dear Lemuel,

> *If you're reading this you know the family home has been left to you as your grandparents' will stipulated upon my death.*
> *I'm sitting here on the eve of history. The first African American has just been nominated by a major party to run for president of the United States. Someone who's given us something that I haven't seen since Dr. Martin Luther King Jr., and the Kennedys: a reason to hope for change, for something better. Not just for African Americans but all people - the World!*
> *Although I don't believe the election of a Black president is likely to happen in my lifetime. I remember the boycotts, sit-ins, and Emmet Till like it was yesterday, but then I never thought I'd live to see **this** day come to pass.*
> *I've been watching you in turmoil over the past few years. I know you chose dentistry mostly to make your grandfather proud. And boy he was, but I believe your true calling lies elsewhere. I know you will probably put the house up for sale, but I hope you don't. I know it's the root of some painful memories for you, but not all bad to be sure. I think the source of everything for which you've been searching, your*

M.T.W. Cruise

purpose, is tied up in that house. Sometimes the very thing for which you are searching is the one thing you can't see. Everything you've experienced in life has brought you to where you are now.

Have you ever looked up the definition of your middle name?

<u>Sphere</u> - n. a solid geometric figure generated by the revolution of a semicircle about its diameter; a round body whose surface is at all points equidistant from the center.

I know your father gave you that name in honor of one of his idols, Thelonious Sphere Monk, but its roots have a far deeper meaning. No matter how far you travel in life you are inescapably tied to the center of this family. You have a lot to say to this world. I know in the end you'll find your place in it.

Lovingly,
Aunt T

2
Giant Steps

Stepping through the front door of his grandparents' two-story Georgetown home brought about a peace and contentment he hadn't known in a long time. The house was warm and comforting like an old familiar chair.

Everything in it from fixtures to furniture had remained virtually unchanged from when he was little - right down to the framed Scurlock portrait of his grandparents that remained prominently displayed on the entryway table among various other family portraits.

Lemuel and his sister had to fight "tooth and nail" to have even the most minor updates installed. They were the last of their friends to get cable television. A dishwasher and microwave were out of the question.

Aside from the dated furniture, the house had been well-maintained. But for the dust that had accumulated over the past few years, the house was in good order. It would bring a handsome price.

By the 1870's, Black Georgetown residents could boast among themselves laborers, porters, barbers, blacksmiths, ministers, cobblers, carpenters, nurses, teachers, a grocer, two policemen and a fireman, to name just a few. Only three decades earlier Black Codes had prohibited Negroes from obtaining business licenses and restricted them to primarily unskilled occupations.

The Black community within Georgetown continued to flourish well into the early 1900's, until the Old Georgetown Act of 1950 swiftly sealed the fate of most of its Black residents. Many were economically unable to comply with new zoning restrictions, higher taxes, and mandatory renovations. Many relocated to other areas of D.C.

Lemuel's grandparents had been fortunate enough to be able to stay and tough it out. Now their P Street home sits in one of the most prestigious and sought after addresses in the city. The area was once a thriving African American community known as Herring Hill.

His parents, Royce and Nina, struggling musicians, had moved from their Dupont Park apartment on D Street in the southeastern section of the city into his grandparents' Georgetown home. They converted the home's old carriage quarters into a garage and upstairs apartment.

M.T.W. Cruise

The house itself held a prominent place in the family's history. During the Civil War, Lemuel's great-great-grandfather, Thornton Taylor, a slave, had been pressed into service as a teamster and wheelwright in the Confederate Army. He fled with the Union Army to the safety of D.C., protected under the Contraband Act.

Family folklore recounts that Thornton assisted in the rescue of countless slaves who risked their lives to cross the Potomac River seeking the tunnel that fed into the basement of Halcyon House (named for the mythical Halcyon bird for its power to calm the winds and waves of the seas) on Prospect Street.

In some instances, a false bottomed carriage was commandeered to transport runaway slaves from the Halcyon House tunnel to a vault in the Mt. Zion cemetery until arrangements could be made to get them to safety. Thornton and other "friends" of the movement, Negro and white, had successfully helped many escape to Pennsylvania, and then on to New York and, finally, Canada to freedom.

3
Time Out

If Lemuel was going to put the house on the market there was a lot that needed to be done. First, he'd have to clean out personal effects. This was as good a week as any. He had closed his office for the week to get his aunt's final affairs in order. Asia had offered to lend a helping hand but this was something he felt he had to do alone.

He began with his sister Amel's room. Vintage Michael Jackson posters were plastered all over the walls the same as they had been the day she graduated from high school and moved away to college. This made him smile. To this day she had a soft spot for Michael, her all-time favorite. Her love of Michael had begun when the family had gone to see the Jackson Five at the Shady Grove amphitheater when she was just five years old.

Amel was like that about every aspect of her life. She knew what she liked and what she wanted and never strayed from it. A trip to New York with their father to see the Broadway play *Dream Girls* when she was twelve had sparked her fascination with architecture.

He and Amel would often drive up and down Wisconsin and Massachusetts Avenues in their father's Delta 88 Oldsmobile and marvel at all the intricate embassy buildings.

She went on to graduate from Howard University's architectural program. Her final project was to design a mausoleum. It was so original and well-designed that she caught the attention of one of the top architectural firms in the country. She's the firm's youngest junior partner at thirty-nine years of age, and resides in Manhattan.

Just down the hall from Amel's room was his. First to catch his eyes were the albums stacked on the shelf by his bed. Flipping through them brought back memories: Parliament; Ohio Players; Mother's Finest; Earth, Wind, & Fire. Of course you couldn't be a native of D.C. without the Unifics, William Devaughan, Blackbyrds, Chuck Brown, and Trouble Funk, in your collection.

There was a special section for jazz. Classics like *Giant Steps*, *Ah Um*, and *A Night in Tunisia* were staples, but it was Miles Davis' *Kind Of Blue* in which he had virtually worn a groove.

Eagerly removing the album from its sleeve, careful only to place his fingers on the album's outer edge as his father had instructed him when he was little, he placed it on the turntable.

M.T.W. Cruise

With all of today's technological achievements you still couldn't beat the warm, rich sound of an old fashioned LP - the days when album covers were works of art.

Turning on the receiver, then turntable, he placed the needle on his favorite selection, *All Blues*.

He remembers the very day he had fallen in love with Miles' infectious trumpet. It was the same day he had experienced his first crush.

He was in the sixth grade. Angie was the new girl everybody was talking about. She hadn't been in his class but all the sixth grade classes had lunch at the same time, followed by recess.

She had been jumping rope on the blacktop with some of the other girls. He and a few buddies were playing basketball on the same blacktop.

When he got home from school that day he raced up the stairs, barely saying hello to his grandmother, to his parent's loft apartment to check out any albums his father might have left for him. "Homework assignments" his father had called them. *Kind of Blue* was on their modest kitchen table affixed with a note: "Lem, check this one out! Dad."

Lemuel liked to put on his favorite pair of metallic green Koss stereo headphones and lie across his bed. He could tune everything out and lose himself in the music.

The melodic riffs of *So What* had immediately pulled him in but it was the infectious refrain of *All Blues* that had enveloped him and explained completely, and in no uncertain terms, all the jumbled up feelings he had felt but couldn't vocalize.

From that day forward he had become a true student of the art. He hungered for everything jazz. His young mind was like a sponge as he spent countless nights reading the biographies of all the jazz greats, Miles Davis in particular. He had totally immersed himself in as much of the culture as he could. He had pressed his parents for trumpet lessons. They had been reluctant to oblige. The musician's life was a hard one with many temptations paved along its path.

For months after reading Mile's account of his own introduction to the trumpet, Lemuel would fill his cheeks with uncooked grains of rice as Miles had professed, spitting out one grain at a time from pursed lips in order to mimic the proper lip formation with which to blow the trumpet most effectively.

Ascending the stairs that had led to his parents' loft apartment was difficult. The loft was a veritable museum. It had remained virtually untouched since his parents' presence.

Lemuel sat at the kitchen table as he had done countless times growing up. Memories began instantly flooding back. Familiar aromas were still embedded in every nook and cranny of the kitchen walls.

He smiled inwardly as he recalled the time his father secretly captured his mother's seductive rendition of *Fever* on his little two-track Realistic home recorder. She had been washing the breakfast dishes one Sunday morning and singing while she worked, as she commonly did.

Music of every type had played 'round the clock. Aside from jazz, there was James Brown, Nat King Cole, Sam Cooke, Gladys Knight & the Pips, Dionne Warwick, and Johnny Mathis, to name a few. His mother had always been partial to the tenor sax of Motown, but Ray Charles was her all-time favorite. He had garnered a special section in her collection.

His parents' love of music was contagious. He remembered donning a suit for an elementary school talent show performance of Smokey Robinson's *Tears of a Clown* when he was six years old. His dad always took plenty of film footage and pictures. He had forever immortalized the performance with his trusty Super 8 camera.

The late night jam sessions had been Lemuel's favorite. Friday and Saturday nights were the best. When they didn't have a gig, his parents loft apartment had been the gathering spot. Though practice sessions took place in the garage, the kitchen had been the center of activity. All the musicians knew they were sure to get a good meal at Royce and Nina's place.

Nina loved to cook almost as much as she had loved to sing. Her fried chicken, cooked to a golden crisp perfection, and homemade biscuits were her specialty. She always used to joke that she could tell when the chicken was done by the sound of the sizzle in the grease. Plenty of Texas Pete and Tabasco hot sauce were always on hand.

Sidney "Big Sid," good friend and fellow musician, always had a pot of greens simmering on Nina's stove, seasoned with ham hocks and a cheesecloth sack of his own secret blend of seasonings.

Royce always had his Teac TCA 40 reel-to-reel at the ready to record practice sessions. He and the other musicians, Slam, Irving, Cozy, Bix, Big Sid, Buddy, Red, and Cecil, would laugh and talk of old days.   Lemuel had loved to sit in on these late night chats.   They were better than any history lesson taught in school.

They often re-hashed the time they had to pass the proverbial hat to bail Big Sid out of jail. He'd been roughed up and thrown in jail for the night for being in South Beach Miami after dark without having the required work card with him.

Similar incidents had befallen Sammy Davis, Jr., in South Beach and Miles Davis at the Birdland Club in New York.

In those days, Black musicians and entertainers were required to obtain work passes to perform in the white sections of cities, but they weren't allowed to stay in the hotels in white areas.

In Miami, most Black musicians stayed in the Black section called Overtown, at the Sir John Motel. They would often come off their South Beach club sets and follow-up with all night jam sessions at the Sir John. Even a few of the white musicians would make their way to the Sir John after hours.   Dave Brubeck was common among them.

Cecil "Mr. Fine and Mellow" liked to talk of the time Billie Holiday performed at the Patio Lounge.

Cecil was from Baltimore, and had lived down the street from Billie on South Durham

Street as a child. His very first job had been running errands for Billie's mother at her short-lived restaurant, East Side Grille. Billie's mother and, shortly thereafter, Billie had ultimately relocated to Harlem, but Billie was still a "home girl."

Cecil and Royce had created the Out Front Quartet jazz band during their freshman year of college in Richmond. They frequented the various D.C. jazz clubs on weekends. Cecil would always, somehow, manage to get them in and even coerce club owners to let them play a set from time to time.

On this particular evening, at the last minute, Royce had had the good fortune to be in the right place at the right time when Billie needed a last minute replacement for her drummer during her second set.

Afterwards, Billie and her band hung out. Billie, who was a great cook in her own right, persuaded the owner to let her into the kitchen. Her specialty was Chicken Cacciatore. She and Nina, who was now the Out Front Quartet's soloist and Royce's girlfriend, fixed up a big feast. They stayed up until the wee hours of the morning eating, drinking, and swapping stories. Sadly, this was one of Billie's last D.C. performances. She died just a few years later.

M.T.W. Cruise

Cecil was an easy-going and friendly kind of guy. He had played a mean bass. But he was also a compulsive gambler with a bad drug habit. He was later stabbed to death after trying to run a hustle at Chester's Pool Room over on 11th and New York Avenue in 1975.

Lemuel relished these bits of history. The weekends couldn't come soon enough. On the nights when they were away, he would listen to his father's collection of reel-to-reel session tapes.

M.T.W. Cruise

Wednesday, January 13, 1982, had been rather uneventful. Schools had been closed yet another day due to heavy snowfall. It had snowed all night prior and was still coming down the next day when he had kissed his mother and shook his father's hand for the last time. They had an engagement in New York at the Lennox Lounge in Harlem.

Later that evening and on into the next day, it had been all over the news. Air Florida Flight 90 had gone down into the Potomac River after crashing into the 14th Street Bridge, just after take-off from National Airport. As fate would have it, Royce and Nina, stuck in the snowy bridge traffic, had been taken with it.

The news was at a standstill with live action footage of the rescue and recovery efforts of the flight's few survivors being pulled from the icy depths of the Potomac.

Lemuel never picked up his trumpet again. It still sat perched atop the very shelf in his room from all those years ago.

4
Weevils in the Wheat

Just off from the living room was the library. It was the nucleus of the house. Lemuel's grandfather had been the keeper of the family's history and an avid collector of African Americana. He had collected thousands of books, many of them first and second additions, pamphlets, newspaper clippings, and memorabilia pertaining to African American life in the United States and abroad.

Lemuel's eyes fell upon the vast collection of rare titles: *Instruction for the Treatment of Negroes*; *Poems on the Abolition of the Slave Trade*; *The Slave: or Memoirs of Archy Moore*; and, *The Negro in the American Theatre*.

Whenever his grandfather traveled he would sniff out off-the-beaten-path book stores and private estate sales to see what he could find in the manner of African American history.

On the wall atop the desk was a framed theater announcement of an 1856 performance of Ira Aldridge, billed as the African Roscius, showcasing his lead in the Shakespeare play *Merchant of Venice*. His grandfather had produced the winning bid on it at a charity auction of a private New York collector.

On the opposite wall hung another of his grandfather's most coveted possessions: the frayed, handwritten pages of an 1891 speech given before the annual American Historical Association by W.E.B DuBois, obtained at the same auction.

But of all his grandfather's possessions he was most proud of his family's history. The family's history had its own section of shelves dedicated to it, all in precise, ascending order, beginning with the family Bible. Over 100 years old, it had been handed down through the generations, beginning with Lemuel's great-great grandfather Joseph Wyatt.

Following the Civil War, the American Bible Society had set about the task of providing newly freed slaves with an education and a Bible. Many African Americans were trained as colporteurs and distributed the Bible door-to-door. A colporteur's visit was a special event in the African American home.

In some cases, African Americans traveled several miles to obtain a Bible. Many preferred to purchase one rather than receive it as a gift.

The Bible was not used, solely, to recite scripture but oftentimes to teach reading. It was the primary repository of family births, marriages, and, deaths.

Lemuel had been well-rehearsed by his grandfather on family history and pressed upon to ensure that it was carried on to future generations.

His great-grandfather, Marcellus Yateman Wyatt, was given his name by his father Joseph, a former slave. It bore the surnames of former owners so that each successive generation could trace his steps. Marcellus had beaten the odds and followed the northern sojourn of Negroes after the Civil War to the city and carried out life as a successful businessman in the tonsorial trade.

His grandfather, Marcellus Hamilton Wyatt, was a Howard University trained dentist who had dedicated his life to the service of others on the battleground of the civil rights movement.

His father, Marcellus Royce Wyatt, had forged his own path as a jazz musician.

For ease of distinction, the two latter Marcelluses were called by their middle names.

The three Marcellus men were shining examples of perseverance and ingenuity. They were the backbone of Lemuel's paternal ancestry of which he was proud to belong.

M.T.W. Cruise

The centerpiece of the library was the Koken barber chair that had belonged to his great-grandfather.

Sitting in the chair and looking down at the foot plate embossed with the Koken company name, Lemuel fondly recalled the countless haircuts and teeth that were pulled while sitting in that chair in this very room.

Browsing the wall-to-wall shelves of books and old family relics, each item told a story in the family's history. Lemuel casually plucks off a book from the family history shelf, *Weevils in the Wheat,* a collection of ex-slave interviews conducted in the late 1930's by the Federal Writers' Project, and opens it to the earmarked page.

———

M.T.W. Cruise

II

Name: Mrs. Hattie Wyatt Freeman (b. ca. 1837)
       Hampton, VA
Interviewer: unknown
Date of Interview: 1937

"I was born on de ole Wyatt plantation in Gloucester, VA. Upton Plantation it was called. Let's see, I was born in - oh 'round 1837, so I guess that'd make me about 100- hee hee- I done lived a long time chile. Des ole eyes seen a lot. Watcha wanna know 'bout?

Plantation life? Well I guess da Wyatt plantation was one a de two or three larger ones in Gloucester. Master John come from a long line a money. Dey come from de old country - England. Master John never did have to lift a finger. He inherited de place from his daddy an so on. Dey was a family a oystermen. Dey owned one a de biggest oyster canning factories in Bena.

De main house was a beautiful brick mansion with great big white pillars out front an ivy growing all up 'round de sides. It overlooked de York River. It was a big plantation so naturally it took a lot a slaves to run it. De slave quarters were located on its own section a de plantation back a de main house. Little two room cabins, one row after another, kinda like rows a corn. An' de whole plantation was closed in by a four foot rock an shell wall dat was built by de hands a de slaves themselves.

Dar were some slaves who worked de fields an some who worked in de big house, you know do de cookin' an cleaning - dat sort a thing. If you worked in de main house, you stay in de house in de servant's quarters so you on hand to take care Master John and Miss Ann. If you worked in de fields you worked sunup to sundown, everyday 'cept Sunday. If you worked in de main house, you worked every day 'cludin' Sundays, but Master John would allow half de house servants to attend church with him an Miss Ann. See so dat way dere be enough servants left in de house to prepare de Sunday supper. Dey would go in shifts, half one Sunday an de other half the next Sunday which is more den us field hands could say 'cause we won't allowed to go to church. Too many I guess.

Some owners would allow dar slaves to have a sorta make-shift church a dey own down in de quarters, but most didn't. Slaves would still find ways to have some type a church or prayer meetin' late at night in one a de quarters but you had to be real careful not to make too much noise or you risk gittin caught by one a de overseers. Dar quarters wasn't too far from de slave quarters, so you had to be careful.

Master John wasn't too harsh. He was young an livin' de carefree life when his daddy died an left him de plantation to run. I was just a little girl when dat happen. I don't remember ole Master too much. His name was Henry. Master John didn't have no momma. She died when he was just a little thing. He was raised by de house servants mostly. He didn't have no sisters nor brothers neither. I was tole his momma an daddy had a boy baby 'fore Master John was born but he was sickly right from de start an didn't live too long. Dey say Master John was right sickly too when he was born an dey didn't think he was gonna live but he fooled 'em and pulled on through.

Master John was de apple a his daddy's eye. He was treated like royalty. Dey 'spose to have been 'scended from de ole country. Master John never wanted for a thing. Had de latest clothes styles. Yessir, his daddy would have 'em shipped special from over in France or somewhere. Master John had de bes clothes, de bes schoolin'. He was spoiled by de house servants, too. An 'cause he didn't have no brothers nor sisters, he had his pick a little slave chillun to play with an keep his company.

When ole' Master died, Master John was still a young man. He wasn't really ready to run no plantation, he was still havin' fun. His father must a known it too 'cause he left de plantation operation to his brother Master William, who had his own big plantation to run over in nearby

Mathews County. Ole Master left it so Upton be Master John's to run when his uncle saw fit for him to run it.

Master John didn't pay dat no never mind 'cause dat meant things could go on just like dey been. He didn't have no 'sponsiblity an he could stay in town for weeks at a time drinkin' an runnin' wit different girls. Master John made his rounds in de slave quarters too. Dar got to be quite a few little light skinned babies running 'round dar.

Well, dis went on for a few years. Master John's uncle got tired a waitin' for him to grow up an take over de plantation. Well, de family thought it was time for him to be gettin' married an settlin' down. It didn't look right for a man his age, he must a been in his thirties by now, to still be out dar having a good time, not married an all. His uncle tried to reason dat Master John could get married an still have his little fun on de side but dat he couldn't manage two plantations much longer. Master John wouldn't hear it but his uncle finally put his foot down an tole him he would either stop all his foolishness, get married an take on his 'sponsiblities like a man, or he'd have to leave de plantation. Master John didn't want to hear dis 'cause dat meant no more easy life, no more fine clothes, no more good food. You know dat meant no more fine women.

So, Master John gave in an agreed to settle

down an marry. He married his twenty year old cousin, Miss Ann. You know dat type a thing was common in dose days. Dat way see dat ole money was assured to stay in de family. Well, he married Miss Ann. She always been crazy about him from de time she was little. Dis was her first marriage, too. Even though she was twenty she was still a naïve little girl in most ways. She was crazy about Master John an I think he loved her too but more like a brother loves a sister than a husband loves a wife.

Things went on as normal for a while. Master John took over de plantation free and clear. Slave life wasn't too harsh. Master John was pretty easy with his slaves long as you didn't cut up. Some a da overseers was mean as dirt but Master John had de final say an it wasn't common for him to whup his slaves. If he had a slave dat kept running away, he just sell him farther down south somewhere. 'Course dat was worse than whippin' sometimes, 'specially if you had family. If dey sole you down to de deep south, chances are you wasn't never gonna see yo loved ones no mo. But Master John, he was very easy natured most a de time.

Missy Ann, she was real mean, specially to de house servants. De more Master John stay away, de meaner she got. She was crazy too. De more Master stay away the crazier she got. She took to doing things to keep him at home. She'd take to hidin' things, like pieces a china or jewelry an blame it on one a de house slaves. She'd raise all type a commotion, have Master John searching all over for her stuff dat never was stolen in de first place. Den she took to havin these cryin fits a hers till finally Master John don't stay away from home no mo. He would go to town to take care of his business affairs an come right back home. Missy settled down for a while an things was normal again. Well, dat only solve half a Missy's problems 'cause like I tole you before, Master John was partial to de slave women, too, an had some chilluns already. Master John thought if Missy had some chilluns maybe it would take de focus offa him, but Missy never could have no chillun of her own. De grown-up slaves felt Missy Ann was right pitiful.

In those times, it was common for a master to have children by his slaves. Everyone knew not to ever say who de father was. Even though everybody knowd it, you never say. I was just a little thing but that's one a de first things you learn. Well, Master John had plenty a little nigger chillun runnin 'round but this one, he was de spittin image a Master, you didn't have to say it. Master John even took partial to him 'cause of it. He would give little Joseph clothes, even made him his personal body servant. Well, it didn't take long befo Missy notice de 'semblance too of this honey *colored slave. Did everything she could to punish little Joseph's momma. Had her sent out to de fields. Tried her best to punish de momma, 'cause she know Master John wouldn't let her lay a finger on little Joseph.*

One night in de middle a de night, I hears all dis commotion. Slaves running 'bout waking de rest a de quarters. De main house done caught fire. At dat time didn't have no fire truck an' hoses like you do now. De best you had was a horse drawn water wagon an most cases by de time it got to de fire it was too late. De slaves had a 'sembly line from de river to de house, passing buckets back an forth to put out de fire. Couple of de slaves tried to get into de house to try an 'rouse Master John, but Missy done barricaded all de doors an windows so dey couldn't get in. By de time dey did get in it was too late. Master John and Missy done burn up, cludin' everyone else in de house.

Well, after dat Master John's relatives come an sell off what was left, slaves included. Most was sold to different places. I was sold to a plantation a little farther south in tidewater - Hampton. Met my husband here. Been here all de rest o' my life. Reckun' I'll die here.

Naw su, don't know whatever 'came o' little Joseph. Never saw him no more. Dem times, slavery times was tough times.

1
The African

"Blow your Trumpet, Gabriel.
De talles tree in Paradise,
De Christian call de tree of life."

Born around 1835 in Gloucester County, Virginia, on the Wyatt plantation, Joseph was seven years old when his life was irrevocably altered. He has fond memories of his mother. He can still see her face, her voice forever etched into his brain.

Celia had sheltered him as best she could from the grueling life of slavery. The two would lie on their pallet at night in their tiny servant's quarters, their backs to each other for warmth. She would captivate him with talk of the far away home of their ancestors. Joseph would press his cold feet firmly against the backs of his mother's legs as she talked with pride about her great-great grandfather, the African, Momodou, and the Wolof tribes.

Momodou came from generations of *guewels* - storytellers. He played the African drum, the tama, and accompanied the tribal king.

M.T.W. Cruise

Celia told of the great old Baobab tree under which Momodou would sit as he told of the village births, deaths, marriages, battles, and more.

The Baobab tree which nourishes its community with shelter, leaves, and fruit had presided over the remains of their ancestors for generations.

Momodou warned of the dangers that lay ahead in the trusting of white men who came bearing gifts of salt and rum.

One day, after suffering defeat in a rival war, the women and children of Momodou's tribe were given as a gift to the rival tribe leader. The men were sold to Portuguese traders and held captive on a small patch of land, a short distance off the shore of their homeland, to await their fate. Each was fitted with long chains attached to heavy metal balls around their necks. Any slave contemplating leaping into the water to make his way back home would surely sink to his death.

Momodou was made personal servant of Don Tristan, on his expedition to establish a permanent colony in La Florida. Soon after the fleet's arrival in New Spain, a great *hurakan* swept up out of the ocean, destroying most of the fleet and provisions.

As the months dragged on, the colonists, desperate to try and eke out an existence, vulnerable and almost out of provisions, moved farther inland in search of Indian villages for food.

One day, as the settlers were once again forced to go in search of food, Momodou escaped along the Alabama River. He was taken in and harbored by the Creek Indians with whom he lived, learning their language and ways of survival.

He fell in love with a beautiful Indian princess, named Liley Red Eagle, and the two lived as man and wife and had many children.

Celia was a house servant who had conceived Joseph by her master, John Wyatt.

Though master John had other slave children, Joseph was the caramel carbon copy of his father, right down to his hazel eyes. Master John, whose wife had been unable to bear him children, was intrigued by the boy's inquisitive nature.

Master John's wife, Ann, resented the resemblance and objected to having Joseph and his mother in the house as constant reminders of her husband's indiscretions. Celia was ultimately sent out to the fields to appease her.

For the first time since birth, Joseph was separated from his mother. He became body servant to his father. His pallet lay at the foot of his father's bed in his personal chambers.

The Wyatts were master mariners and owners of the largest oyster canning factory in Bena, seated in Gloucester County.

The brushed brass encased mariner's compass atop the mantle above the fireplace in his father's room had immediately drawn Joseph. He would lie on his pallet at night and marvel at this foreign object.

Master John delighted in explaining to Joseph the compass' use and its importance to the mariner's trade. He pointed out the pole star, the magnetic star that "shows the way," and its magnetic stone, the lodestone.

Joseph hadn't slept in his father's chambers the night of the big fire. He had been sent to the quarters. His father had taken one of his slaves to his bed that night. This had pleased Joseph immensely. He would be reunited with his mother, if only for the night.

He had been awakened in the middle of the night to a blur of commotion as slaves and overseers rushed to quell the fire that would ultimately claim the lives of all who were trapped inside the main house.

After Master John's death, the plantation was disbanded and the slaves sold off, regardless of family ties. Joseph was never to see his mother again.

M.T.W. Cruise

He was bought by the owner of the 600 acre Shefford plantation in bordering Mathews County. The plantation housed one of the biggest shipyards on the tiny, 94 square mile county.

Shipbuilding had long been passed from fathers to sons, dating before the Revolutionary War. The seemingly endless forests of Live Oak trees that dotted the area made it an ideal location for ship construction. Many a Continental navy ship had been built upon the middle peninsula.

Plantation patriarch Beaumont Shefford Yateman had inherited Shefford from his father who died after a jagged piece of oyster shell lodged in his throat, resulting in a fatal infection.

Joseph became the body servant of Beaumont's son, Philip Marcellus Yateman. He learned all manner of the shipbuilding and transport businesses from Philip and proved a worthy apprentice.

Philip founded a lucrative transport company in Gloucester County where the two plied their trade along the Chesapeake Bay. Joseph built his own bateaux with the portion of earnings he was allowed to keep.

2
Freetown

"Dere's a meeting here tonight.
I take my test in Matthew and by de Revelation.
I know you by your garment,
Dere's a meeting here tonight."

Joseph was allowed to retain a portion of the pay he received from the various odd jobs he was allowed to perform. This provided him a sort of independence and by the age of twenty-five, he had secured $650 of his own money to purchase his freedom.

He built a modest home and merchant store of his own on Horseshoe Bend in Scottsville. The store gave him a profound sense of pride, but it was guiding his bateaux up and down the canal that gave him the most pleasure. He would guide the hogshead laden bateaux up the James River and Kanawha Canal en route to Richmond, where it would be unloaded and reloaded with goods for his mercantile store. The mariner's life was in his blood.

The town of Scottsville spanned the counties of Albemarle, Buckingham, and Fluvanna. Horseshoe Bend owed its name to the horseshoe shaped land mass of the town of Scottsville that encircled the northern swell of the James River.

The southernmost section of town, near the canal entrance, came to be called Freetown by the locals due to the fact that many of the businesses and bars located along its stretch were owned and operated by free Blacks.

Well before the Civil War, these businesses had catered to soldiers and seamen. Ferries docked daily, loading and unloading hogshead barrels of supplies.

The majority of these free Blacks resided in a settlement called Free Hill on the Fluvanna County side of Scottsville. Free Hill was a colony of former slaves who lived on land given them by their former master upon freeing them. This small group of former slaves grew into a tight-knit community complete with little houses, yards, and gardens.

The nucleus of the community was the log meeting house where Pastor Langhorn ministered dutifully to his flock of Huckles, Mayos, and Duncans, to name a few.

To the east of Free Hill was the Free Hill burying ground where many of its inhabitants were laid to rest under an arbor of peaceful shade trees.

M.T.W. Cruise

Descendants would inhabit Free Hill for generations to come.

Haverhill Plantation was located on the southern bank of the James River in Fluvanna County, Virginia. Its massive expanse included a granary, tobacco house, stables, blacksmith shop, carpentry shop, cobbler shop, two ice houses, several barns and storage buildings.

Its palatial grounds were overgrown with wild persimmon trees. Its fruit, commonly called "possum apples," was picked upon ripening and turned into persimmon ice cream in the summer. A special treat for all to enjoy.

Julia was the third generation of her family to be born on the Haverhill plantation. Her father, Noble, was a skilled cobbler. He, along with his brothers Isaac and George, oversaw the production of all the plantation shoes. They even filled orders from other area plantations.

Julia's mother, Nellie, was the head cook in the main house. Her kitchen skills had been handed down to her by her mother. Her special delicacy was persimmon cobbler and homemade persimmon ice cream. Julia took up training as head cook and quickly proved to be every bit as able a cook as her mother.

Julia's family, like many of the Haverhill slaves, lived as an intact family. Slave housing was substantial with well-built plank flooring, glass windows, and a fireplace for heat and cooking.

Though one of the largest slave owners in the county, Haverhill Plantation owner, Master William Alpheus Whitlock, believed in allowing his slaves a place of their own to worship. Joseph was to oversee its construction.

Julia was the sweet and refreshing breeze blown his way each day as she was set to the task of bringing the laborers their midday meals during the chapel's construction. Joseph could not have foreseen that he would later secure her freedom, nor that the two would be "married" in that very chapel.

Master Whitlock looked kindly upon Joseph. He held more progressive notions than most of his contemporaries and looked favorably upon any man, slave or free, who dared to better his lot through resourcefulness.

Though, admittedly, he couldn't run his massive plantation without slave labor, he supported emancipation and was, at one time, vice president of the American Colonization Society, which spearheaded efforts to colonize emancipated slaves to Liberia.

In theory, he considered slaves capable of moral and educational equality and self-government but deemed it impossible for the two races to live, work, and interact alongside each other peacefully due to the centuries of persecution that Negroes had suffered at the hands of whites.

The Deportation Act of 1806 required slaves to leave the state within a year of obtaining their freedom. Slave owners feared newly freed slaves would incite insurrection among slaves. The Act sought to discourage liberal slave owners from emancipating their slaves.

Ultimately, Whitlock rationalized that he needed his slaves as much as they needed him. Rarely were his slaves ever whipped or dealt with harshly. He couldn't understand the mind set of harsh owners.

In light of his views on the education and self-governance of slaves, he and his like-minded wife educated slave children in a little brick schoolroom on Haverhill. Slaves were given a basic education or taught a trade of some sort. This was a risky endeavor since Virginia law forbade and punished anyone involved in the education of slaves, considering it likely to cause malcontent among slaves and ultimately lead to insurrection.

Indeed, public outcry against the teaching of slaves was so vigorous that Whitlock suffered many public confrontations and was the victim of a severe beating on at least one occasion.

M.T.W. Cruise

3
Southern Claims Commission
(Before the Commissioner of Claims)
Claim of Joseph Wyatt
May 25, 1874

Scottsville, VA

After walking up the narrow dirt path that led to his house and up the three short wooden steps to the porch, Joseph removes his muddy boots before entering the house. It was an end of the day ritual he performed out of habit more than anything. Julia had never allowed him to enter the house with them on. He would beat them clean once the mud was dry just as she'd always done.

The boots were especially muddy today. Earlier that afternoon he had been knee deep in mud and muck trying to beat back flood waters as they, yet again, surged from the James River.

Ascending the narrow hallway and entering the small kitchen always comforted him at the end of the day. He sat at the tiny kitchen table before a covered plate of chicken and homemade rolls his oldest daughter, Virginia, had prepared, just as her mother used to do.

At twelve years old she had long ago shed the demeanor of a child to fill the void her mother had left. He could still feel Julia's presence even though she'd been four years gone.

It had been close to the war's end on March 10, 1865 when the Union Army, led by General Sheridan, had encamped in Scottsville.   The soldiers had apprehended one of his tow horses on the James River and Kanawha Canal off Bouldin's Landing, about five miles from Scottsville, before taking up camp nearby.

Fear of a Union raid had caused some residents to flee. The canal was vulnerable as the Union Army sought to disable the confederacy by wrecking the canal, destroying locks, and blasting dams.   Many feared their businesses would be burned. Many Negroes fled with the Union Army. Joseph, a free Negro, had stayed.

The location of merchant businesses and bars along Horseshoe Bend on the canal was ideal for the Union Army to get supplies and provisions such as shoes, blankets, flour, sugar, and salt, all of which, the commanding officers assured, would be compensated at the war's end.

Joseph willingly gave the soldiers free access to his store and to whatever food and provisions of which they were in need. Though he was born and reared in the south, his sentiments lay with the northern cause.

Julia prepared and delivered food, water,

and modest medical attention to the men, daily, during their five-day encampment.

The rosy rash on Julia's and little Marcellus's tongues and necks had appeared shortly after the Union Army had gone on its way. They had contracted scarlet fever.

During their sickness Julia, not wanting the other children or Joseph to contract the disease, had mustered up all the strength she could to tend to their son. The two stayed quarantined in specially prepared quarters just off the kitchen on the back porch. The only one allowed admittance was old Doc Porter.

In her weakened condition, Julia kept vigil over Marcellus, day and night. A small 12x12 opening was cut into the bottom of the back door of their "sick" room and sealed with plastic, where Julia would receive food and water from Joseph.

She would leave soiled diapers and linens for him to take up. The diapers were to be burned and new ones cut from fresh cloth.

Marcellus had grown stronger with every day that passed. In Julia, scarlet fever had manifested itself into rheumatic fever leaving her heart severely atrophied.

Eventually, she was unable to perform even the most trivial of household chores. Unable to stand for long periods of time, Julia took to relegating the duties of the house to their three girls from the makeshift wooden wheelchair that Joseph had fashioned out of pinewood and old cart wheels.

Most of the work fell to Virginia who took up the slack with deft and ease that her mother had left.

In the end, Julia had been confined to the bed, no longer able to sustain the strength required to sit in the long discarded wheelchair. One summer night, content with the knowledge that she had adequately prepared her family to live without her, she died.

Joseph would make the journey to Richmond on horseback to the war commissioner's office to file his claim for compensation.

He had secured the necessary letter from his former owner attesting to his character and the date he had secured his freedom. Two of Julia's uncles were to go along to confirm his loyalty to the union cause and to bear witness to the supplies that had been furnished to the Union Army during their encampment. He thought himself well-prepared.

Any southerner who suffered loss at the hands of the Union Army could file for compensation from the war commission. However, Negroes, especially ex-slaves, were subjected to a specific set of inquiry questions: strict proof of ownership and property title; former owner's name and residence; proof of date of freedom and how it was obtained; what business you followed; how the money was obtained to purchase freedom; and, testimony as to loyalty to the union cause.

Answering these questions and providing proof proved challenging for many former slaves. Former owners were sometimes deceased or unable to be located. Many records were destroyed during the war. Ultimately, only a fraction of claims was approved and out of those few approved, even fewer were approved for ex-slaves.

The money, if any, Joseph received as compensation from the war commission would do little, however, to fill the void his life had sustained from the loss of his soul mate and trusted companion.

———

III

The next item to catch Lemuel's eye was a worn, leather-bound scrapbook of newspaper clippings. It had belonged to his great-grandfather, Marcellus Yateman Wyatt, a prominent Vinegar Hill barber in Charlottesville, before urban renewal had forever altered its landscape.

The scrapbook of clippings from the respected Negro owned publications, *The Richmond Planet* and *The Reflector*, along with the *Charlottesville Chronicle*, the *Richmond Dispatch*, and the *Fredericksburg Free Lance* newspapers, chronicled life and events of the citizens of Charlottesville and surrounding areas through the 1940's, ending abruptly a few years before Marcellus's death in 1946.

Marcellus had died long before Lemuel was born, but he held fond memories of the many childhood summers spent visiting the Charlottesville family home, then inhabited by his great-aunt. He would sit on the front porch and listen to his grandfather, great-aunt, and parents talk of old times.

When he tired of that he would hop on his skateboard, his basketball tucked under his arm, and play in the parking lot of the nearby neighborhood school.

Perusing the various societal pages announcing church group meetings, social club gatherings, and wedding announcements, the

Wyatt surname is commonly found.

In addition to the societal pages and announcements were articles chronicling events that his great-grandfather had felt important enough to hang on to. Lemuel is ashamed to admit to himself that he'd never actually bothered to read any of them.

Taking a seat in the Koken barber chair, he began by reading a collection of clippings from the *Richmond Planet* detailing an infamous Charlottesville murder trial.

1
Charlottesville, VA
March 29, 1890
The Planet

One could say that the Wyatt & Allen barbershop was a "planet" all its own, at least after hours on Wednesdays and Saturdays. The shop sat at 213 W. Main Street in the heart of Vinegar Hill's Negro business district.

Negroes gathered after regular business hours not only for a cut and shave but also for camaraderie as they strove to keep abreast of community goings-on and to hash out political issues.

Colored men from all economic backgrounds patronized the Wyatt & Allen barbershop, especially on Wednesday evenings when the weekly edition of the *Richmond Planet* rolled off the presses. On Saturday evenings men brought their sons for their Sunday church trim-up while getting to the heart of current political and community issues. In this time-honored tradition of male bonding, the playing field was level. In the Wyatt & Allen barbershop everyone's voice was weighted equally.

Like most southern businesses, barbershops were segregated. Most of the Negro owned barbershops on the Hill catered to a predominantly white clientele. There were a few that catered to an all Negro clientele. Negro barbers had to be well trained in cutting all types of hair.

The origin of the Negro barber began during slavery when white masters apprenticed their slaves to white barbers to learn the trade and earn money for their masters.

After slavery, the profession was fostered by Negro barbers who ensured its continuance through apprenticeships. However, unlike their white counterparts, their concern was not only teaching the trade but education as well. Many took the young apprentice into their homes and fed and clothed him.

Negro barbers flourished during Reconstruction. One didn't have to know how to read or write to learn the barber trade. A relatively young boy could start out as an apprentice and work his way up to journeyman status, earning full wages and, eventually, master barber and own his own shop.

Leading white citizens enjoyed being pampered by Negro barbers in what they felt was a mostly non-threatening role of service.

Black and white relations in Charlottesville were mostly cordial. For the most part, Vinegar Hill Negroes enjoyed a self-maintained lifestyle with little interference from white society. Businesses ran the length of Main Street, beginning in the downtown area up to the University of Virginia.

Black businesses occupied the north side of Main Street and white businesses the south side. Charlottesville's white population routinely patronized Vinegar Hill's Negro businesses.

Outside of the Negro owned businesses that patronized whites and the Negroes who ventured across color lines to work as domestics, the two groups had little occasion to intermingle.

Every Negro barber knew he had to tamp down the political rhetoric in the presence of white customers. Occasionally, racial divisiveness would flair over some local or national event. There was the occasional white patron who would openly air his grievances. Emotions ran deep on both sides.

Though the Wyatt & Allen barbershop served a white clientele during the day, it was well-known among Charlottesville's Negro citizens that Wednesday and Saturday evenings were unofficially reserved for their patronage.

Negro patrons came from all over Charlottesville and the nearby areas of Scottsville, Ivy, and Richmond. It wasn't uncommon for Negro luminaries of the day, Booker T. Washington and W.E.B. Dubois among them, to stop through for a cut and shave. It had garnered the reputation as the place to hear a valid cross section of the Negro populous.

On one such Wednesday in 1890, James H. Hayes, Negro defense attorney in the Muscoe murder trial, stopped in before returning home to Richmond.

William Muscoe had been twice convicted for the murder of a white policeman in Charlottesville on New Year's Eve two years prior. The officer had attempted to arrest Muscoe on W. Main Street for petty larceny. A struggle had ensued that left the officer dead. Muscoe fled and was later captured and taken to Richmond for safekeeping until the trial. He was convicted and sentenced to be hanged.

Hayes argued for and was granted a new trial on grounds of technical error. Nevertheless, Muscoe was convicted a second time.

The talk in the barbershop on this particular evening centered around the fact that Hayes had secured a thirty-day respite from Governor McKinney in order to allow him time to prepare his papers in the State Supreme Court of Appeals to argue once more for a new trial on the grounds that the jury was wrongfully instructed by the judge; the prisoner was not convicted on the actual evidence; and to request a change of venue.

Muscoe had narrowly escaped a lynch mob after local whites had learned of the delay and organized an attack on the Charlottesville jail where he was being held. Monticello guards, fire, and police units were dispatched to protect the jail and the prisoner as he was whisked away to a Lynchburg jail for safekeeping and order was restored.

Hayes withstood a barrage of attacks to his personal character and unorthodox legal tactics by the prosecuting attorney. The state prosecutor quickly found himself outmatched and resorted to prejudicial tactics once he felt that he couldn't win on the legal facts alone.

The feelings within the Charlottesville community were palpable. The tension was felt in the streets, stores, businesses, and the courtroom. The case was closely followed and played out in both the white and Negro press.

Although Attorney Hayes argued a sound case in Muscoe's defense before the State Supreme Court, the second appeal was ultimately denied.

Muscoe was to be hanged April 21, 1891.

2
Marcellus

Born amidst all the chaos and uncertainty of war in 1862, Joseph and Julia had bestowed all their hopes and aspirations on their only male child, Marcellus.

Julia had had the benefit of an owner who believed in a basic education for his slaves, acknowledging that their freedom was inevitable.

She had taught all of her daughters to read and write from the family Bible. They, in turn, had helped to teach their little brother.

Though Joseph had never had the opportunity for a formal education, he had always hungered for knowledge. When the Scottsville Freedmen's School was established, they had all attended. He had been a firm believer in education for all of his children.

During monthly business trips to Richmond, Joseph would retrieve the previous month's newspapers from one of his suppliers who would sell them to him for a fraction of their cost. Sometimes he was able to secure a few of the Negro publications.

Marcellus would read them front-to-back to his father. The two would sit up late nights discussing various topics. They often debated Booker T. Washington's and W.E.B. Dubois's opposing positions on obtaining Negro equality and education.

Joseph often stressed the importance of education, not merely a trade, as the best chance for Negroes to further their lot. A trade was merely a means to an end.

The destruction left in the wake of the Civil War had severely stifled trade up and down the James River and Kanawha Canal. Trade along Horseshoe Bend never returned to pre-war levels. Later on, the railroad system of conductors and porters replaced packets and bateaux for transport of goods and leisure travel.

Marcellus picked up the barber trade through an apprenticeship with a local barber. He was twenty-one years old when he left his childhood home in Scottsville to follow the influx of Negroes from rural environs to various cities and towns in search of work. He felt it was the city that offered Negroes the best opportunity for independence.

3
Vinegar Hill

The steady migration of Negroes to Charlottesville continued steadily after the Civil War. Emerging Jim Crow sentiment had brought forth the need for economic independence. Negro owned businesses addressed the rising demand by Negroes for a varied assortment of goods and services. By the 1920's, these businesses encompassed the prime of Vinegar Hill, developing it into the center of Negro residential and social life.

There was a Negro owned drugstore, shoe repair shop, clothing stores, barbershops, poolrooms, restaurants, a physician, a dentist, and a mortician. The Blue Diamond night club played jazz.

There were no hotels for Negroes, but many residents took in out of town boarders to earn a little extra income.

Though Vinegar Hill was comprised of many Negro owned businesses, a fair amount of Charlottesville's Negro residents traveled to the predominantly white areas of the city to work as domestics. Many were employed at the University of Virginia as maids, cooks, washerwomen, and orderlies in the University's hospital.

M.T.W. Cruise

However,   Charlottesville's   Negro community was a self-preserving one. They came home to their own neighborhoods and patronized their own businesses. Consequently, Negro owned residences and businesses flourished.

The areas two main churches, First Colored Baptist on 7th & W. Main Streets and Mt. Zion on Ridge Street, were the focal points of the community for both spiritual and social guidance. Both held morning and evening services on Sundays to accommodate domestic workers who otherwise wouldn't be able to attend. One could, and often did, attend church all day on Sundays, only retiring to the home in the midday for supper.

Negro chapters of fraternal orders and benevolent societies: Odd Fellows, Masons, Eastern Star, and Elks, were heavily populated. There were various social clubs: 3V, Literary, Lucky Thirteen, and Secret Twelve, to name a few. Federated women's clubs such as the Phyllis Wheatley Club were also available.

These clubs and societies were necessary, not only for social outlet, but more important, they provided a means of addressing the needs of the community which the local government did not.

Charlottesville's Negro residents were identified by various monikers. Some were members of the Four Hundred Club. The Four Hundreds were free-born, as opposed to being "shot-free" or freed by the war. They were self-educated Negroes who were able to secure well-paying jobs which had enabled them to purchase $400 plots of land. They comprised the upper echelon of Charlottesville's Negro elite.

Other prominent Negroes lived on Fifth Street in an area that came to be known locally as Starr Hill. The area acquired the name due to the many prominent Negro Vinegar Hill business owners who lived high upon the hill. Starr Hill residents took pride in the fact that they owned their own homes. No one rented.

Both groups were very visible in the community and stood as powerful role models, setting the tone for social and civic responsibility in the community. Most had pulled themselves up from meager beginnings.

M.T.W. Cruise

4
Lula

At eighteen years of age, Lula took work as a live-in domestic servant in Charlottesville while earning her teaching certificate from the Rappahannock Industrial Academy. Though she somewhat regretted leaving her tiny hometown of Cuckoo in Louisa County, she armed herself with her Bible and her tattered copy of Webster's blue-backed speller and set out with a sense of purpose and independence.

Lula was the youngest of three siblings. They were the products of their white slave owner father and his slave. Their mother died when Lula was seven years old, leaving them in the care of their aunt.

Lula's maternal grandmother, Louisa, a slave, had fled north during slavery with her common-law husband, Orpheus, a free Black, amid increasing danger for runaway slaves and free Blacks, after the Compromise of 1850 Fugitive Slave Law.

Under the protection of the Vigilance Committee, they safely made their way to Ontario, Canada. Orpheus found work as a carpenter and Louisa, a dressmaker.

After the Civil War, they returned to the

United States, settling in Richmond, Virginia, in an area that was later dubbed the "Harlem of the South." The Jackson Ward area became a thriving, self-sustaining neighborhood of affluent Negro society.

Orpheus was employed as a waiter, then cook, for the Richmond, Fredericksburg, and Potomac Railroad. Louisa quickly found work as a seamstress.

Charlottesville's Negro residents looked to the society pages of the *Richmond Planet* to keep apprised of club meetings, social events, church sponsored programs, entertainment parties, school events, fundraisers, visiting relatives, weddings, sicknesses, and deaths.

It was at the monthly meeting of the 3 V Club that Lula and Marcellus, the club's secretary, met. The two were later married at the First Colored Baptist Church.

Lula retired her rural teaching post after she and Marcellus were married. She was regal in her role as matriarch of the house. She took pride in her home and her family. She was an avid host of the various social clubs to which she belonged.

Hill families took great pride in their homeownership and their manicured lawns. The homes weren't particularly huge and the lawns were relatively small, but everyone took exquisite pride in what they had.

Lula was a firm believer in self-sustenance and delighted in working in her garden. In it she grew tight, neat rows of corn, sweet off the vine tomatoes, cucumbers, beans, and squash. Her own little private "Victory Garden."

Mulberry bushes lined the backyard fence. These she kept pruned and watered. During mulberry season, she plucked the purple fruit and made mouth-watering mulberry pies, cobblers, and jams. Some she sold in her husband's barbershop and some she sold at church and community fundraisers.

She was an excellent seamstress and worked from their modest home to help supplement Marcellus' barbershop income. Their girls always had replicas of the latest styles, fashioned by Lula's able hands.

Sunday was church day. Church was the backbone of the Negro community, aiding in everything from the spiritual and social to business guidance.

Marcellus and Lula were not merely members of the First Colored Baptist Church but active participants. They were firm believers in not only attendance but in cultivating a strong relationship with the Lord and the community through service in the church. They instilled this sense of duty in their children at an early age.

5
Hamilton

As a boy, Hamilton's presence in his father's barbershop was strictly forbidden except after hours on Saturdays when the barbers and other community men would gather to shoot the breeze and discuss issues. His father didn't want him earning money from shining the shoes and sweeping up the hair of white men. Hamilton was to stay focused on his education.

Though the barber profession had provided their family a descent way of life, Joseph and Julia believed education was the gateway to dignity and respect.

They had been able to provide a sound education for their children beyond the eighth grade curriculum that the Jefferson School provided.

Colored families who could afford it paid room and board for their children to go out of town to receive a high school curriculum. Hamilton and all of his sisters received high school and college educations at Virginia State College in Petersburg.

The barber trade was quickly changing. As the white business community began to realize how profitable the tonsorial trade was, white owned barbershops steadily increased.   Barber unions were created to try and invoke laws requiring new barbers to pay dues and pass state exams to earn a certificate before legally operating a barbershop.

This would all but shut out many Negro barbers, most of whom picked up the trade through apprenticeships.

Those who were already in business were not held to these new laws, but it would have a dramatic effect on the future of the business.

What had begun during slavery and viewed as a non-threatening service trade providing the personal grooming of leading white citizens had proved so lucrative a business it had white businessmen jockeying for the upper hand.

By 1896, the Journeymen Barber's International Union of America (JBIUA) sought to invoke a standard of care in the barber trade. This was seen by most Negro barbers as a bullish tactic aimed at the exclusion of Negro and Italian barbers, their major competitors.

Although national membership was open to all, Negro barbers included, local chapters were segregated. The Union as a whole did little to address racism within the organization. By the early 1900's, Negro barbers saw little value in joining.

Marcellus's voice in the community had, at times, irritated some in the white business community. When the Union raised the price of a shave from .10 cents to .15 cents, he let his stance on the issue be known. He refused to join the Union and prominently displayed a sign in his barbershop window advertising .10 cent shaves.

Marcellus was of the opinion that Negro barbers ought to band together to fight the JBIU and preserve their way of life and the integrity of the profession itself. They should, instead, rely on each other for support.

Eventually, Union scare tactics were employed under the guise of promoting hygiene. Though the Union had failed in its initial attempts at lobbying for licensure and dues requirements, many barbers found they had to invest heavily in equipment to meet the new standards for hygiene.

Negro barbers had to remain competitive in order to continue to attract white customers as Americans' appetite for luxury grew. Many came up with enterprising ways to continue to draw influential white clientele. Some provided personalized shave mugs, manicurists, and even stenographers to their customers. Others went to great lengths to invest in modernizing equipment and focusing on creating regal appearance and architecture.

Marcellus was an excellent businessman. He kept his eyes attuned to any business edge, looking to stay one step ahead of the competition.

M.T.W. Cruise

By the end of the 19th century the phonograph was steadily growing in popularity as a means of amusement for the general public.

Marcellus invested wisely in an Edison H coin slot phonograph. Customers marveled at this new technology, paying .5 cents a turn to wind the phonograph's handle and hear George W. Johnson's infectious "Laughing Song."

The Barbieris, an immigrant Italian family, was typical of most immigrant families in America. They were humble, hardworking, and self-sufficient.

Mr. Barbieri followed the ancestral trade of which his surname was derived. He owned a barbershop on the south side of East Main Street directly across from the Wyatt & Allen barbershop. He, his wife, and their son, Angelo, lived in a modest apartment atop their barbershop.

Mrs. Barbieri worked as a maid at the University of Virginia. She rode the bus everyday with Negro women who also worked at the University as domestics. To help make ends meet, she took in work as a washerwoman on the side.

Angelo, was an apprentice in his father's barbershop. He often leered across the street at the Wyatt & Allen barbershop as he swept the front walk.

He resented the fact that most of the Negro

business owners in Charlottesville lived in nice houses, with fenced-in yards, and dressed in nice clothes. His father would admonish him to be patient. Like most of the younger generation, progress didn't occur fast enough.

Once, Hamilton came home from school just as a visibly agitated and mildly intoxicated Angelo pounded away on the front door. He left easily enough but not before letting a few disparaging remarks fall from his lips.

Lula cautioned her son to keep the incident between the two of them. She felt Angelo was harmless enough and feared what her husband might do if he found out. She had good reason to fear if he chose not to let the incident rest.

A few weeks later, Hamilton and his father were approached by Angelo late one Saturday night after leaving the barbershop.

Marcellus cautioned his son to remain quiet and to let Angelo go on his way. He let his anger get the better of him after Angelo, heavily impaired by alcohol, hurled his empty bottle into the front windowpane of the barbershop, shattering it completely.

Marcellus grabbed him by his shirt collar and shoved him up against the side of the building. They stood locked in this manner for what seemed like an eternity to Hamilton before his father turned Angelo loose after all.

M.T.W. Cruise

He later explained to his son that there were "many forks in the road of life and you can only choose one path. One moment of snap decision could forever define the rest of your life."

Though outspoken on issues affecting the Negro community, Marcellus was a peaceable man who didn't try to incite unnecessary friction between the races but rather sought to bring about change through understanding the white man's way of thinking.

Marcellus and Lula would later come to the Barbieris' aid after their barbershop and home were suspiciously set ablaze. They organized a community fundraiser to help set them on their feet again.

The Barbieris would later stand side-by-side with Marcellus and other Negro and immigrant barbers to challenge the bullish tactics of the Union.

With the constant threat of Union dues, licensure, increasing competition, and, finally, the advent of the electric razor which meant that customers could get a decent shave in the privacy of their own homes for free, Marcellus felt his son needed to pursue a more stable career path.

Hamilton gave his future a lot of thought before concluding that dentistry was an area in which he could do well while also providing a much needed service to his community.

Dr. Harris was the first Negro dentist he had ever seen. He had begun his dental career as a traveling dentist on horse and buggy.

Post-Civil War, most Negro dentists lacked the necessary finances to buy equipment to open dental offices. Consequently, this group became known as "street dentists." They carried their instruments with them and performed services in the streets or in patients' homes. Their patient base consisted of Negroes whom white dental professionals were reluctant to treat.

Upon graduating from Howard University's Dental School, Hamilton set up practice in the small town of Fredericksburg, about an hour west of his boyhood home of Charlottesville. He began his practice out of a room in the McGuire Hotel.

To supplement his initial income, he worked as a bellhop in the whites-only Princess Anne Hotel.

Eventually, his practice grew enough to warrant a larger space. He quit his job as bellhop and rented half of the upstairs of the old Gravatt Carriage House.

Armed with his set of dental school books and instruments, book shelf, meager desk, an old Koken barber chair his father had donated (there was only negligible difference between barber chairs and dental chairs), and a few chairs that had been abandoned by a previous tenant, Hamilton thus began his practice.

At the constant urging of his mother to "plant roots in the community and join a good church," he became a member of Shiloh Baptist Church (Old Site).

He knew that efficiency and organization were the key components to any cause, and he was gifted in both areas. He began to lay the foundation of a life of community service.

Howard University Dental School, the fifth oldest in the Nation, stressed service to community and taught its students how to serve the Negro community more efficiently. Aside from the dental curriculum, Howard's goal was to help their students circumvent the challenges they faced as Negroes within their professions.

Hamilton became a member of the local chapters of the NAACP and the Old Dominion Dental Society. Both organizations were committed to breaking down the barriers, social, political, and professional, of not only Negroes but the economically disadvantaged of all races.

While week days were filled with building a budding dental practice, evenings were spent poring over local newspapers to keep up with issues affecting the community and looking for areas where he could get involved.

Hamilton's father had often commented that an effective leader was "well versed on all sides of an issue." This point had been further reinforced by his college debate team.

The University of Virginia's snub of Negro civil rights activist, Richard B. Moore, under the guise of thwarting the spread of communist philosophy, further ignited Hamilton's urgency to get involved.

The University had welcomed many speakers in the past of varied and sometimes controversial platforms, communists among them. Objections to Moore's engagement was most assuredly due to the fact of his having been a Negro.

Moore, who had emigrated from Barbados to the United States in 1909, was a nationally acknowledged speaker. He later joined the African Blood Brotherhood, organized to defend Negroes from race riots and lynchings.

By 1935, he had become an invaluable organizer for the International Labor Defense (ILD), a non-partisan legal defense organization, which spoke out passionately against the ills of Jim Crowism and the evils of capitalism. Moor would later use his influence within the ILD to speak on behalf of the Scottsboro Boys.

After witnessing and being on the receiving

end of racial discrimination in America, Moore along with other Negro activists, was drawn to the Communist Party which had little tolerance for the ideology of segregation.

Though Hamilton was against communism in principal, he could understand its growing appeal to some Negroes.

The Communist Party USA addressed the needs of the Negro community and the issues that the American political system was unwilling to address. Its mantra was that the liberation of one group was essential to the spiritual and physical freedom of all.

It was one of the most active organizations in campaigning against evictions, lobbying for unemployment benefits, and speaking out against police brutality.

Unlike any other organization in America, the Communist Party didn't just place Negroes in positions of power but expelled any members who exhibited racial prejudice. The organization believed that workers should share in the wealth created by the work they did and criticized organized labor's efforts to remain an all-white affair.

It was also quick to attack organized labor's attempts to create division among working class whites and Blacks by inserting anti-Black sentiments.

M.T.W. Cruise

Hamilton firmly believed the democratic process of a government run by and for the people was best as long as it worked to ensure that every group of society was equally weighted and represented.   He didn't believe in the ultimate practicality of a totalitarian political system.

Still, he was inspired by Richard B. Moore. A bibliophile, Moore had collected over 15,000 books and pamphlets on the Black experience worldwide. Like Moore, Hamilton, too, would aspire to amass whatever books, pamphlets, and clippings he could as testimony to the Black experience as a way of ensuring that future generations would gain a better understanding of the ground that had been laid by their forbearers.

———

IV

Exodus 13:21

"And the Lord went before them by day in a pillar of a cloud, to lead them the way; and by night in a pillar of fire, to give the light; to go by day and night."

1
Georgetown
Taylor Wheelwright & Carpentry

"Oh! Go down, Moses,
Away down to Egypt's Land,
And tell King Pharaoh to let my people go."

In 1873, Thornton Taylor brought from Essex County, Virginia to live with him in Georgetown, Washington, D.C., his wife Bettie and their six children.

Thornton was an ex-slave who had been owned by the Hunter family, one of three major slave holding families in Essex County.

He was owned by the younger Hunter sister, Sallie, on the palatial Font Hill Plantation, which was owned by her brother, R.M.T. Hunter.

Thornton was a carpenter by trade. Many families, Negro and white, could boast that he had built their Essex County homes. He had been a teamster and wagon repairer for the Confederate Army before escaping with the Union Army and brought to the District of Columbia where he was safeguarded by Contraband Act. Following the

Civil War he remained in D.C. and found work as an itinerant carpenter.

Having been a pivotal inspection and shipping station for tobacco, the District of Columbia (D.C.) had been at the center of the domestic slave trade. Georgetown had been home to a considerable population of Blacks, slave and free, before and after the Civil War.

When the tobacco trade diminished in the Chesapeake region, the rapid expansion of cotton as the primary cash crop in the Deep South generated a renewed demand for slave labor. Slave dealers and planters sought to capitalize by selling surplus labor in the domestic slave market.

D.C.'s slave trade had been abolished in the Compromise of 1850, angering the bordering slave states of Virginia and Maryland. Many feared that easy access to the District would lead to insurrection. The District's prime location connecting the upper and lower south and providing access to the Potomac River and the Chesapeake Bay, made it an ideal escape route for slaves looking to head north to freedom. Captured runaway slaves were routinely shipped by barge farther south to New Orleans.

In actuality, the Compromise only forbade anyone to bring slaves into D.C. for the purpose of selling them out of state. It was still legal for a

Washingtonian to put his slave up for public auction.

Slave auctions throughout D.C. were common sights in front of such establishments as John Beattie's Tavern on High Street, McCandles' Tavern, and in front of hotels and prisons.

On April 16, 1862, when the District's slaves were first freed by act of Congress, compensating slave owners for releasing their property from bondage, the District of Columbia became a Mecca for runaway slaves and free Blacks, further angering the surrounding states of Virginia and Maryland where slavery continued to flourish. However, owners from these states often hired their slaves out to work in the District, usually a year at a time.

The Taylors' reputation in the community had provided them the friendship of many influential and prominent Negro citizens. Dr. & Mrs. James H. Fleet, and authors and educators, Angelina Grimke and Dr. Anna Julia Cooper were among them. Grimke and Cooper both taught at the M Street School, of which Anna Cooper later became principal.

Dr. James H. Fleet, whose father had purchased his freedom after securing his own, had been a physician by training but a teacher by choice. He, along with two other free men of color, had received their medical education under the sponsorship of the Maryland Colonization Society in exchange for their agreement to emigrate to Liberia upon completion.

Fleet later had a change of heart about honoring this arrangement. His active involvement in the 1835 Negro Convention Movement in Philadelphia had soured his and many others support of emigration.

The Movement had originated to denounce the forcible emigration proposed by the American Colonization Society. It was believed by many that the hidden purpose of the Society was to strengthen slavery by ridding the country of its free Black population; repatriation as a way to avoid slave rebellion.

Instead, the Movement opted for improving the socioeconomic conditions of free Negroes and the denouncement of the continuance of slavery in the south.

Fleet abandoned the practice of medicine and opened a much revered school for free Negro children at which both he and his wife taught.

Dr. and Mrs. Fleet were active abolitionists. They participated in countless local anti-slavery activities helping to raise money for individuals wishing to secure their freedom.

Dr. Fleet died in 1861 before he could see the abolishment of slavery. Mrs. Fleet carried on the groundwork she and her husband had laid.

Like many freedmen, the Taylors lost much of the money they had managed to amass with the failure in 1874 of the Freedmen's Savings Bank. Created by the Freedmen's Bureau after the Civil War, mismanagement had led to its demise.

Friends implored the Taylors to stay and tough it out, pointing out that the American League of Colored Laborers encouraged Negro craftsmen to establish their own businesses and could, perhaps, be of some assistance to someone with Thornton's carpentry skills.

They stayed and Thornton converted their carriage house to incorporate a wheelwright shop: Taylor Wheelwright & Carpentry.

2
Essex County, VA

Englander Ann Bundy emigrated to the United States in 1719 when, on her 16th birthday, her father put her on a ship named the Majestic from the Portsmouth port in Hampshire.

After making the necessary arrangements with the ship's captain and signing the papers that bound her to a term of indenture, Ann Bundy was bound for the New World. Her father was reticent as he hugged and kissed his daughter, assuaging her with promises of a new and better life.

The Thirty Years War had severely depressed Europe's economy. Ann's father was a skilled but out of work blacksmith in the tiny town of Amesbury in Wiltshire, England. Her mother had died when Ann was just a small girl.

Ann's father had been forced to vacate the small plot of land he had farmed. A hard-working and proud man all of his life, he had been reduced to vagrancy. He and Ann moved about the overcrowded cities.

Preying on the downtrodden and desperate, the "soul sellers" who were becoming pandemic across the countryside had spoken of the endless opportunities that awaited all who emigrated to the

New World. On the contrary, the almost twelve week passage across the Atlantic Ocean was anything but majestic.

Ann's father had no way of knowing about the tightly packed bodies kept in holds below the deck without fresh air, weekly rations of bread, foul water, stench, sickness, and death. Nor could he know of the dead bodies, ravaged by hunger and sickness that were routinely thrown overboard during the journey. Of those who did make it to the New World, many died of disease, such as small pox, within the first year.

If passage had not been arranged prior to the journey, immigrants remained aboard until arrangements were made with the ship's captain to pay for their passage.

The typical term of indenture was 4-7 years, at the end of which the servant was paid freedom dues of corn, tools, and clothes.

Ann was indentured to John Perry of Essex County, Virginia, in return for her passage to America. Her term of indenture was subsequently lengthened as the penalty for giving birth to a mulatto child.

By law, her offspring was, thereby, indentured. Mulattoes who were born into servitude were required to serve until they turned thirty-one years of age.

M.T.W. Cruise

Wilhelmina Bundy's marriage, in 1905, to Mercer Taylor, the son of Essex County carpenter, Thornton Taylor, was immediately frowned upon due to his family having been former slaves. The Bundys had been born into indenture but had never been slaves.

When Mercer died of tuberculosis, Wilhelmina fell into a great depression, rarely leaving her home.

She, too, succumbed to the dreaded and much feared disease less than two years after her beloved Mercer, though it was said she really died of a broken heart.

Tuberculosis sufferers were often ostracized from society. In many instances, the only treatment facilities open to Negro TB patients were state mental institutions or, worse, the state penitentiary. Hygiene levels and quality of care were lacking in both. Whites feared the spread of the disease to them through their cooks, nannies, and laundresses. Many died at home alone.

Mercer and Wilhelmina's three children were left in the care of their maternal grandparents. Vashti, was the oldest at six years old, followed by Walter who was four, and Wilhelmina "Winnie," the youngest, who was two years old - mere stair steps.

M.T.W. Cruise

As the oldest, Vashti often bore the brunt of her grandmother, Virginia's frustrations.   Her darker complexion, however slight, often caused friction between the two.

Her grandmother often chastised, "You're just another one of Hunter's niggers." A remark made to slight her deceased son-in-law, borne, in part, out of anger and the blame that she placed on him for her daughter's death and partly out of fear as she sought to keep Vashti on the straight and narrow path.

Virginia, who had reared ten children of her own, was sixty years old when her daughter died leaving her to rear three small grandchildren. She feared that she was too old and tired to give them the proper guidance they would surely need.

In the midst of her new domestic circumstances, she would receive a letter from the War Department, a full month after the fact, informing her of the death of her youngest son, Thomas, in France. He had been yet another casualty of the influenza epidemic that had befallen many soldiers during World War I.

Vashti grew to favor her doting grandfather. She cherished the Sundays when she would sit alongside him through the macadam streets in his horse drawn buggy on their way to church.

M.T.W. Cruise

Knowing elders watched with bated breath as their worst fears materialized. They had been sure the relationship would run its course and the situation would resolve of its own volition.

When Walter announced the news of his intensions to marry Cora, the matter could be put off no longer. Upon learning that he and Cora could not marry because they were, indeed, half brother and sister, he was distraught. Cora was the love child of his father and another woman.

Heartsick and disgusted, Walter left home and took work in D.C. as a bus boy and waiter at the Mayflower Hotel. He later met and fell in love with Peggy who was vacationing on the east coast with her parents.

He hadn't set out to deceive anyone. His fair skin had led Peggy and her family to assume he was white. He found it easy to shed his old life and swap it for this new one. After that, it was easy to concoct the story that he was an orphan whose parents and siblings had drowned in a terrible boating accident.

Walter returned with Cora and her family to California where he later took advantage of the west coast auto boom and established a successful auto leather upholstery business.

There would be brief and sporadic visits by Walter to family throughout the years. A private post office box was established to keep up correspondence.

Virginia was seemingly partial to Winnie who took on the lighter skin tone and features of the Bundys. Vashti was a beauty in her own right, but Winnie was the "stand out."

Winnie had never known her father who died soon after she was born. Susceptibility during pregnancy had led to her mother's sickness. She was just two when her mother died, too young to hold any concrete memories of the mother for whom she was named.

Elders never discussed aloud the circumstances of her parents' deaths. Tuberculosis was not something that was openly discussed. Winnie would be a grown woman with children of her own before she would learn the truth.

At fifteen years old, upon completing her primary education at the little one room Antioch grade school in her hometown of Champlain, she traveled the 40 some odd miles by bus to attend the Fredericksburg Normal and Industrial Institute to complete her high school education.

Fredericksburg Normal and Industrial Institute was organized by Joseph Walker and Jason Grant in 1905 in the basement of the Shiloh Baptist Church. The school provided room and board, therefore, providing service to surrounding counties that did not offer a high school curriculum for Negroes.

Winnie worked as a domestic in the evenings and on weekends at one of the local hotels to pay her room and board.

Though she never gave up her membership at her home church, Antioch Baptist, she began attending the Shiloh Baptist Church (Old Site) where she met, and later married, a handsome and charismatic young dentist named Marcellus Hamilton Wyatt.

———

St. Mark 10:45

*"For even the son of man came not to be
ministered unto, but to minister, and to give his life
a ransom for many."*

1
The Negro in Dentistry

A Negro dental practice wasn't as outwardly lucrative as one might have imagined. At a time when many struggled to make ends meet, oral hygiene was not always a priority. There were those, white and Black, who felt that Negro dentists weren't as well educated a white dentists. Never mind that Negro dentists were required to pass the very same state board exam as white dentists.

Once, as Hamilton waited for his office rent receipt to be written, the white attorney had casually inquired "Out of curiosity, of all the professions you could have chosen, why did you choose dentistry?," matter-of-factly pointing out that, while dentistry was a noble profession, it would most likely prove financially unrewarding for a man of color.

At first, Hamilton had been a little put off by the dismissive forgone conclusion of certain failure. After considering the question for a moment and realizing that no harm had been intended, he responded that it was just something that he thought he'd like to do. There was a lot more he could have said. He quickly realized that this attorney had no way of relating to the urgency and need in the Negro community of having access to professional medical and dental services that they might otherwise have to do without. Failure was not an option and was, in effect, beside the point.

Some white dentists accepted Negro patients before and after normal business hours so as not to offend their white patients. Many refused to even treat Negroes.

Later in life he would recall the conversation with mixed emotions. Indeed he **had** been excluded from the mainstream of dentistry and was rarely, if ever, able to talk with another dentist in town. Early Negro dentists were routinely denied access to new discoveries and information.

A budding dental practice and civil rights causes meant long days and frequent nights away from home. Civil rights activism, though a necessary and worthy cause, didn't pay monetarily. Various groups would often raise funds to help offset travel expenses. Otherwise, you made out the best way you could.

Hamilton was not one to turn a blind eye when it came to the injustices and humiliation Negroes suffered at the hands of Jim Crow. His pragmatic approach often led him to question the impracticalities and ironies of segregation.

M.T.W. Cruise

The Greyhound Bus Station on Princess Anne and Wolf Streets had segregated seating and restrooms. Both were clean and decent. The lunch counter served **all,** however, whites were served drinks out of *green* glasses and Negroes out of *tan* ones. Ironically, all were washed together in the very same dish water.

One day, Hamilton stopped at a local gas station to fill his tank. His friend hopped out to use the restroom and was promptly told by the attendant that he was not welcome to use the facilities. Hamilton turned off the pump at thirteen cents and vowed never to patronize the station again.

Other areas of civil unrest required a more hands-on approach. When Dr. Martin Luther King, Jr. was assassinated, looters from D.C. poured into Fredericksburg hoping to unload the loot they had gotten from rioting. Many of Fredericksburg's angry Negro youth wanted to carry out looting in town.

Hamilton and other area leaders helped quell the situation by calling for cooler heads. A peaceful march was organized down Princess Anne Street from Shiloh Baptist Church (New Site) to St. George's Episcopal Church.

Hamilton used his status as a dental professional and local civil rights organizer to garner access to venues which could further drive his service to the public. When the opportunity and the platform arose, he spoke up. He frequently appeared in the local newspapers speaking out on civil injustices.

In 1967, American Nazi party leader, George Lincoln Rockwell, staged a rally in the city park, during which time a football game, hosted by the all-Black Walker-Grant High School, was to take place.

Hamilton, along with other local NAACP leaders, notified local FBI officials of the potential situation. The rally was ultimately moved back to take place a few hours prior to the game. FBI officials and police were dispatched to be on hand in the event that things turned violent.

A Free Lance-Star article detailing the rally captured a picture of Rockwell waving a shotgun over his head with an inset of Hamilton, arms folded, looking on.

2
Winnie

Winnie was often left to tend to the home front. An equal and willing participant to the cause in her own right, she was the perfect complement to Hamilton.

Growing up in Essex County had taught her nothing if not resourcefulness. Jars of homemade preserves, fruits, and vegetables lined their cellar shelves. In this way, Winnie held the household finances in check.

She supplemented the household income with the unequalled culinary talent she had acquired from her maternal grandmother. Her deviled crabs, soft-shelled crabs, and sweet potato pies were local favorites.

The children would load their toy wagon with their mother's homemade delicacies and distribute orders to local restaurants, both white and Black-owned.

Winnie relished the evenings when she could sit on the porch of her best friend Viola. The two would catch up on local gossip while sipping lemonade and playing "gin rummy." They shared a kindred bond of social status and familiarity.

Viola's husband, a once prominent and

successful local barber, had squandered the family's income on drink, eventually losing the shop and the family's main source of sustenance. They swiftly fell on hard times. Viola struggled to make what little money he did manage to bring home stretch to feed and clothe their twelve children.

Keeping to the old adage that charity begins at home, Winnie would often gather the clothes her children had outgrown and whatever leftovers she could from her own table and take them to Viola so they would have a little extra.

Conversely, life in Winnie's own household steadily favored the better. Hamilton was able to build up an adequate practice which met most of their needs and a few extras.

They were one of the first family's in the neighborhood to get a television. Although the garish roof-top antennas were unmistakable, you didn't want to make it too widely known that you owned a television or your home would be constantly flooded with curious onlookers.

3

Royce

Growing up in the small town of Fredericksburg, the child of one of the town's few Negro professionals and outspoken civil rights leaders had its advantages, but it hadn't been all roses. Many was the time Royce came home as a youngster with a blackened eye, a direct result of verbal taunts.

In class he would occasionally overhear the nasty remarks of fellow classmates, "My daddy said he wouldn't go to Dr. Wyatt; he hurts you." They undoubtedly made sure he was within earshot of these proclamations.

Some of the teachers were no less tactful. Once, after turning in a report that he had labored over for a week, his teacher had casually concluded that he had not written it. His father was summoned to the school to attest to the fact that his son had indeed written the report on his own.

Still, Royce held fond remembrances of the town's easy and gentle life. Playing marbles on the front stoop with friends and swimming in the Rappahannock River were among his fondest recollections.

If you were colored there were no public

pool facilities. His mother had strictly forbade swimming in the river, but all the kids did it. The favorite point of entry was in back of the Shiloh Baptist Church (Old Site).

It was not without its dangers. The river was shallow for certain distances before giving away to a channel that dropped off onto a shelf. A few kids had drowned tempting fate, including a younger cousin.

The "Five Hundred" block of Princess Anne Street was a constant draw. Known locally as "Little Harlem," the area was mostly comprised of Black-owned businesses. There was Tate's Drug Store, the Curtis Department Store which housed Wright's Barber Shop in its basement, Baylor's Barber Shop, and J.H. Myers' Confectionery store, to name a few.

On Saturdays you could spend the better part of the day at the movie theater watching old "shoot 'em ups." You could watch the same reel over and over as many times as you wanted. Fifteen cents afforded you a ticket, a soda, and a candy bar.

The pool halls also provided entertainment. Older guys always hogged the tables, but if you hung around long enough an argument was certain to break out, or a fight if you were real lucky. Once, Royce even witnessed a stabbing.

M.T.W. Cruise

There were two popular beer joints, Little Harlem and the Paris Inn. The latter was owned by the father of Royce's best friend, Alfonso. There were rooms for rent upstairs. Alfonso made his pocket-change by taking pictures and patrons, developing them in one of the unoccupied rooms, and selling them.

Royce also liked to frequent the building which housed his father's dental office. His father shared the upper office space with a prominent Negro attorney. The bottom half was occupied by Miss Martha's hair salon on its backside and Pop's Records in the front. Royce would spend hours in Pop's thumbing through stacks of records.

Pop's place was kind of small and there was only one listening booth. Pop constantly complained that Royce was tying up the booth from paying customers.

There were two Negro owned hotels in town. They sat directly across from one another on Princess Anne Street between Lafayette Blvd. and Wolfe Street.

They were the Rappahannock Hotel, called Brown's Hotel by locals because it was owned by Arthur Brown, a local undertaker, and the McGuire Hotel, owned by Dr. Webster Lee Harris.

They were the largest Negro hotels in the state; a rare stopping place for Negro travelers on

Route 1 between D.C. and Richmond. Both Brown and Harris had prided themselves on their establishment's listing in the Negro Motorist Green Book.

Published by Ford Motor Company, the Green Book was an invaluable resource to Negro travelers. It provided the names and addresses of Negro-owned and Negro-friendly establishments in various cities across the country.

Royce would often join his father in the evenings after dinner to listen to the men gathered out front of McGuire's long front porch. Taxis would sit alongside the curb to pick up fares. He had loved to hear the men with names like "Big Toc" and "Little Toc" talk of old days, politics, and relationships.

In the summers, stores often set up televisions in their windows or on sidewalks to lure customers. Royce and his father had watched the Joe Louis/Ezzard Charles fight this way. A small crowd gathered around the tiny television, set up by an appliance store in the side parking lot, to watch the fight. The "Brown Bomber" had lost the fight that night.

A colored child could keep himself within the safety net of the Negro community for only so long. The blight of Jim Crow found its way in eventually. As Royce grew older he became more aware of and affected by these discrepancies.

He had to walk several miles pass the white public school to get to Walker-Grant, the only colored high school.

If his mother, Winnie, wanted to shop in nice department stores, she had to take her seat in the rear of the bus to Richmond to 2nd and Broad Street, commonly called Deuce Street, the shopping district.

Some found colorful ways to get around this indignity. If the bus was crowded, Winnie's fairer skinned cousin, Peola, would often sit up front in the section reserved for whites and pretend not to know her until they got to Richmond.

To add to the indignity of having to ride in the back of the bus, Negro patrons weren't allowed to try on clothing in the major department stores like Thalhimers and Miller and Rhodes.

Some indignities were more subtle. The WWII homecoming parade was telecast on all the major television networks. Negro units, who were present in the parade, were inconspicuously edited from the televised airing. The NAACP helped to bring to light such injustices.

As a teenager, Royce often shadowed his father to various NAACP events and strategy sessions. The two Shiloh congregations, old and new site, remained a united front on issues of civil rights and public safety. Local civil rights leaders often met at Shiloh (New Site) to discuss strategies.

After Emmet Till's murder, Royce accompanied his father, and other local NAACP officers, to one of the Richmond churches to hear Emmet's mother, Mamie, speak of her son's gruesome lynching in Money, Mississippi.

Royce's father had passed along a sense of pride and duty to his children. There was a time to turn the other cheek and there was a time to get in the trenches and fight. However, he always added the caveat that "not all Black men are your friends and not all white men are your enemies."

The February 1, 1960 sit-in at the Woolworth's in Greensboro, North Carolina had helped bring national attention to the debate over integration in public facilities.

Likewise, on February 22, 1960, scores of local college students staged a sit-in at the Richmond Thalhimers Department Store to protest their whites-only lunch counter.

In its aftermath, thirty-four students had been arrested and jailed. The students became known as the Richmond 34.

The students were ultimately bailed out with funds raised by the NAACP and university officials, some of whom put their own homes up as collateral.

M.T.W. Cruise

After the 34 had been arrested, the remainder of the students, Royce among them, were told to turn around and return home. Their goal had been achieved. The plan had been to force an arrest and get it publicized so that the validity of the law could be challenged in the courts.

The three major Fredericksburg store chains, Woolworth's, W. T. Grant, and People's Drug, steadfastly held to their refusal to serve Negroes at their lunch counters. Local leaders helped to organize a sit-in among the youth.

Each worked with the students to prepare non-violent protests. The students were to dress neatly and were cautioned not to touch merchandise.

No real violence was encountered but various other tactics were employed to discourage protesters. The W.T. Grant store roped off an area and placed blankets in the seats. Protesters knew better than to touch or be accused of stealing. Other stores opened their lunch counters for a couple of hours a day to patronize white customers.

Under pressure and with the whole world watching, by July 30th, W. T. Grant and Woolworth formally announced the desegregation of their lunch counters. The remaining hold-out, People's, soon followed.

———

M.T.W. Cruise

VI

Jazz Goes To College

1
Why Don't You Do Right

Royce played the drums in the high school marching band. His father had inadvertently helped to foster his love of music. Nat King Cole, Duke Ellington, Ella Fitzgerald, and Lena Horne had provided the soundtrack as his father worked for as long as he could remember.

At Pop's Records, there was always the latest stack of rhythm and blues and jazz to peruse. Once Royce stumbled upon a Max Roach album he knew at once he wanted to play the drums. By complimenting a song's melody with the drums, Roach had shattered musical conventions. It was because of him that drumming was no longer just keeping time. It was music.

Royce lay in his bed in Kingsley Hall the better part of the week trying to shake off a bout of winter flu. He was unable to attend classes or to practice with the band. He was even unable to join his other dorm mates in the student lounge to watch, *"The Untouchables."*

The annual winter talent show was Saturday. Though he was still rather weak, by Friday he was feeling better. The show had to go on. After all, the drummer is crucial to the band. By Saturday morning he was feeling better still. He spent the rest of the day rehearsing for the night's show with the band.

They called themselves The Out Front Quartet. Its members consisted of Melvin, tenor saxophonist, Cecil, on horns, himself on drums and vocalist, Deena.

Deena had Ella Fitzgerald's vocal range and the good looks that complimented her vocal skills. All the band members had a crush on her at one time or another, but Deena wasn't the kind of girl you could tie down. She liked to spread her attentions around.

The song selection was an old blues hit by Lillian Green called *Why Don't You Do Right*, later popularized by the sultry Peggy Lee.

Royce could recall the 78rpm Bluebird label spinning round and round on the RCA Victrola that had belonged to his grandmother. The song had been his mother's favorite.

At the last minute, Deena, too, had succumbed to the flu and had to bow out. It was too late to rehearse with another singer even if they did find someone to replace her. It looked like the show wouldn't go on after all.

Melvin, who always had a long list of tricks in his repertoire, told them to leave it to him. He knew just the right person. The band members were skeptical but vowed to show up ready to go on as planned.

Royce had been the last one to arrive. In his rush out of the dorm, he had forgotten his "lucky" drum sticks and had to double back to retrieve them. He stumbled through the back stage curtain just as the band was introduced. Standing before the microphone was a Dorothy Dandridge look-a-like. Nina's powerful rendition brought the house down. He was mesmerized.

His reverie was abruptly interrupted by the arrival of Nina's boyfriend back stage.

Marlon was the campus football star and fraternity hunk to boot. All the ladies swooned whenever he came into a room. He was always in the campus paper.

Noticeably irritated and seemingly unmoved by Nina's performance, he couldn't wait to whisk her away. An argument ensued. In the end, Marlon had left Nina alone in tears.

M.T.W. Cruise

2

Meet Me at Mary's Place

Nina was the youngest of four and the only girl. During the week, her father lived in New Jersey working as the driver for a prominent white family. Her two older brothers joined the armed forces during World War II. When her remaining brother, Robert, left home to attend college, she, alone, was left to shadow her mother as she tended to the family farm of chickens, pigs, cows, and vegetable garden.

Norman was a small country hamlet about an hour's drive south of Richmond - a sleepy little village made up of farmland owned by former slave owners and former slave descendants.

Historically, poor whites and poor Blacks had worked alongside one another. Jim Crow would later put a strain on race relations. The town's Main Street adhered to the same rules of segregation as most other southern enclaves.

Nina was often cautioned by her mother not to "let them seat you at the counter" when she would have occasion to enter the Main Street drugstore. Nina sometimes gave in to temptation.

At times, her fair skin and naiveté were used at her expense. Her age relative to most of her classmates usually made her the youngest in a

M.T.W. Cruise

group of older and wiser girls.   They would occasionally coerce her into sitting at the "whites only" lunch counters for kicks.

Black teens and young adults looking for entertainment usually had to travel to neighboring counties to socialize and listen to music. Horseshoe Inn and Cross Creek, named for the tiny wooden bridge that crossed a creek (many a drunken patron had mis-stepped his way into the creek below) were two such establishments.

To those in the know, there was one local haunt known simply as "Mary's Place," named for the buxom Black woman who owned it.

The small, clapboard structure was an anomaly at the end of a tiny, winding dirt road in the middle of nowhere, surrounded by a seemingly endless forest.   No name plate adorned its entryway.

On any given Friday or Saturday night regulars would enjoy the soul food dish of the day, cooked by Mary herself, as the "jukebox" cranked out the hits of day.   Sounds reverberated and invariably shook the rafters, causing the structure to tremble on its foundation until well into the early morning hours.

Just a few months shy of her sixteen birthday, Nina graduated valedictorian of her class at George Washington Carver High School. That fall she enrolled in a small, historically Black University in Richmond.

English was the solid, sensible major her high school English teacher had encouraged her to pursue. Theater and the performing arts were her real passions. She not only had a flare for dramatic prose, but she had a strong voice.

On their first date, Nina and Marlon walked the one and a half miles from Lombardy Street to Leigh Street and over to East Broad, Richmond's shopping district, to take in a movie.

On their return home, they stopped by the Silver Coach for a couple of BLT's and cokes.

The tiny wood-framed enclosed structure was as old as the University itself. It was the closest off-campus eating establishment that provided easy access to students within a short walking distance to and from campus.

Just past dusk, as they walked casually back to campus enjoying the cool evening breeze, a car, unnoticed at first, passed them before stopping a short distance up the road and turning around. Slowing as it neared them, a round of verbal assaults and racial epithets were hurled like bullets out of lowered windows. The car's inhabitants demanded to know what this "nigger" was doing walking down the street with a white lady!

Marlon quietly cautioned Nina to remain calm. They would keep walking and ignore the taunts.

The driver and his cohorts, determined to be heard and seemingly unable to provoke the desired reaction, promptly exited the vehicle. Marlon pleaded with Nina to run and not stop until she was safely back inside her dorm. With reservations, but no time to think it through further, Nina took off running towards campus while Marlon fled in the opposite direction.

Nina couldn't sleep at all that night, sick with worry about Marlon. Her concerns were fully warranted. He sustained a horrible beating but had walked away with his life after having finally been able to assure his attackers that Nina was indeed a Negro; a light-skinned Negro.

The beating he had taken on her account had endeared him to her, but their relationship had been tumultuous from the start. Marlon had likened her to some prized trophy to be worn on his arm. He liked the attention she garnered until it had started to encroach on his own accomplishments and threatened to overshadow him. It seemed there was only room for one campus star.

M.T.W. Cruise

3
He Will Break Your Heart

Royce couldn't get Nina out of his head. He wasn't going to let a little thing like Marlon stand in his way. It was obvious that he didn't know how to treat a lady anyway. Marlon was too in love with himself to love Nina. Royce decided he wouldn't waste any time. He would strike before she had had the chance to forget him.

Flowers and candy weren't his style. He knew in Nina he had found a soul mate. It seemed they had been cut from the same mold.

The next day as they ate their lunch at the College Inn, the campus grill, he pressed his bandmate, Melvin, for as much info as he could. Melvin shared with him the fact that Nina worked part-time in the afternoons doing secretarial work for the University president. Royce decided he would scout out the location before he made his move.

As luck would have it, Nina's work space sat right by a window overlooking a small courtyard that was seldom frequented by students. Royce knew just what he would do.

For the better part of a week, just before she was to leave for the day, Royce came to the courtyard and serenaded Nina with a smooth rendering of Jerry Butler's hit, *He Will Break Your Heart.*

At first, she was flattered, but only mildly amused. By day four, she had started to soften. Royce's persistence paid off when, on the fifth day, instead of packing up her belongings for the day and promptly leaving for her dorm, Nina sauntered on around to the little courtyard instead.

4
D Street

Without word to either's parents, Royce and Nina drove to Annapolis, Maryland and eloped the weekend before graduation. After graduation they rented a Dupont Park apartment on D Street in SE, Washington, D.C.

Royce found night gigs at some of the local clubs around the city. A few paid but most did not. He reasoned that the experience was priceless and would one day pay off.

The gigs were sporadic at first. They filled in up and down the U Street corridor at various clubs like Bohemian Caverns, Casbah, Bengasi, Chez Brown, and Manny's Lounge whenever a band was in need of a last minute drummer or vocalist. Then, later, as semi-permanent replacements for various musicians.

They ran the D.C. "chitlin" circuit of clubs, but also New York, Miami, and every city in between. They were going to be the next Max Roach and Abby Lincoln.

When the 1968 riots threatened to overtake the city following the assassination of Dr. Martin Luther King, Jr., Royce and Nina, along with other musicians and business owners along the U Street corridor, helped in any way they could to try and restore calm.

Nina was temporarily employed at a consulting firm downtown. She had to remind her albeit well-intentioned, white employer that "those people" were "her people" after he had cautioned her to steer clear of the area.

The rioting that ensued destroyed many businesses and clubs, but the Florida Avenue Grill and Ben's Chili Bowl both survived unscathed. It was rumored that the Grill had survived because its owner had sat atop the roof with his shotgun to deter looters.

In between club dates and civic responsibilities, Royce and Nina were blessed with two children, Lemuel and Amel. Both were born at Providence Hospital.

The Shrimp Boat fed Nina's cravings during both of her pregnancies. The Shrimp Boat was a long-standing tradition that had begun in college when their friend, "Big Manny," would take orders and drive to D.C. and back to Richmond with food. He would take out his pay for gas in food.

Royce's parents, Hamilton and Winnie, later relocated to Georgetown into the inherited home of Winnie's paternal ancestors.

Hamilton, a retired dentist, took a board

position at Howard University's Dental School, his alma mater. Having been a one-time president of the Virginia State NAACP, he kept up with the civil rights causes he'd fostered in Fredericksburg.

Equally active as deacon and Christian Youth Leader at the Fredericksburg Shiloh Baptist Church (Old Site), he felt at home in the Shiloh Baptist Church of D.C.

During the Civil War, the Union Army had used the Fredericksburg Shiloh Church as a make-shift military hospital. Union soldiers had helped some of the slaves and free Blacks, who sought refuge from rigid fugitive slave laws, escape to Washington, D.C., where they established a new Shiloh Baptist Church.

Winnie felt that her grandchildren were being reared in an unstable environment. She worried that Royce and Nina's life of constant traveling, late nights, and the revolving door of musicians at all hours was not the stable, nurturing environment in which to rear children. Their apartment had been broken into on more than one occasion.

The final straw occurred when Nina's weeding ring was stolen. They had mistakenly thought it safeguarded from potential theft by keeping it in a little baggie in the ice box.

At Royce's urging, Nina would remove her ring when they had engagements. He thought it was good public relations for the audience to believe she was unattached. Nina hadn't exactly applauded this tactic, but she had gone along with it.

Much to Winnie's relief, they were finally convinced to move into the family home in Georgetown and convert the old carriage house into a loft apartment.

———

VII

"Education is not the filling of a bucket but the lighting of a fire."

William Butler Yeats

On the eve of the first African American presidential nominee, Lemuel's children seemed light years away from slavery. In actuality, they were only four generations removed from it.

Ironically, in today's technologically advanced society it seemed people had lost a connection to their past and to one another. Today's youth seem detached from their history with no ties to their heritage.

Lemuel looks up at the African proverb inscribed on the placard atop the door of the library.

When an old man dies it is as if a library has burnt down.

Just as his African ancestor, Momadou, his grandfather had been the designated "story teller" responsible for carrying on their family's oral traditions dating back generations. His grandfather had impressed upon him the duty of each successive generation to instill a sense of pride in one's culture and the importance of carrying on its traditions. Lemuel didn't want that history to die with him.

African Americans are unlike any other culture. They are detached and in many ways, disconnected from their African ancestors. Like orphans, they have no concrete ties to their forbearers' cultures and traditions. Lemuel was often dismayed at the disparities, especially among the African American social classes, of what he felt was the devastating loss of cultural pride.

Just the other day, his sixteen year old son had casually remarked that his white friends sometimes used the word "nigga." In response to his utter shock at this revelation his son had proclaimed that it was "no big deal" and it "didn't mean the same thing it did a long time ago." His son had thought he was making too much of it.

Only a few weeks ago the headline news story of the week was about a group of white teenagers who had taken to cruising desolate African American communities, menacing its residents and shouting racial epithets. This joy ride ritual had ultimately escalated into the beating death of an innocent African American man who had the misfortune of being in the wrong place at the wrong time. The horrific crime had been captured on a nearby security camera.

The assailants, now facing federal charges of a hate crime, insisted that though they had shouted racial slurs, they were not racists but had simply targeted the area because it was a lower income community. Shockingly, many of their African American classmates pledged their support.

This had further reinforced, in Lemuel's

mind, the decreased sensitivity of today's African American youth and their inability to relate to the protest marches, sit-ins, and lynchings that their ancestors had to endure. This detachment, he felt, directly correlated to the lack of the competitive drive required to compete in society on a global scale. If one has no connection with the past and present, it's impossible to stay connected to the future.   One must study his past, even its blemishes, to know his future.

He reflected on the words of a "Go-Go" dancer named Glory he used to know in the eighties. She would carry a journal around with her and write in it all the time. He once asked her what she was always writing in her journal to which she had responded, "I write everything that happens to me, good and bad. I don't leave anything out."

To say Glory had endured a rough life would be putting it mildly. She had run away from home when she was fifteen and fallen victim to the streets before landing a job as a dancer at the This Is It Club.

Writing in her journal was a way of keeping a handle on her life and trying to make sense of it. It was cathartic, even if she, herself, didn't understand why she was driven to do it.

Lemuel had not thought of her in all these years until just that very moment.

M.T.W. Cruise

While he believed it was commendable to teach children not to see color with regard to a person's ability or character, he felt it was a disservice not to acknowledge a person's heritage. In order to be a truly cohesive and inclusive society we must teach our children to embrace and celebrate each other's diversities, not pretend they don't exist.

With the advent of and ever expanding availability of social and media networking, we are now able to connect to other cultures in ways that have never been possible. We can now educate the masses and celebrate other cultures. One can live in New York and speak out against injustices occurring in California or anywhere in the world. There is no longer the need to travel to the site of the injustice to be heard or taken seriously.

It dawned on Lemuel that his grandparents' home stood as a testament to the lives, sacrifices, and contributions of his family; an endearing legacy of their lives that should not be diminished with time. However, it was not merely a repository of African American history but **American** history.

He realized that he couldn't sell the house. Somehow, it seemed wrong to upset the history in it. Aside from the historic artifacts the home held, it had played a part in the Underground Railroad. It should be deemed a historic site.

Suddenly, it felt as if a veil had been lifted

from Lemuel's eyes, a weight removed from his chest. Excited and brimming with ideas, he sat at his grandfather's desk and began formulating a plan.

He would request a meeting with the principal of Dunbar High School, along with the District's superintendent and school board officials. Given its historic significance in the community, Dunbar seemed the most logical place to start.

The prestigious Dunbar High School was originally named the Preparatory High School for Colored Youth and then simply referred to as the M Street School. Its name was ultimately changed to Dunbar High School in 1916 after the renowned poet and playwright Paul Lawrence Dunbar.

It had maintained such an impeccable academic record that Negro parents from surrounding areas in Virginia and Maryland had been known to move to the District specifically so their children could attend.

The majority of Dunbar's students weren't comprised of elite Negro society, but were the sons and daughters of laborers, housekeepers, and cooks. Yet, the school continually boasted high scores on standardized tests.

Among Dunbar's distinguished alumni were many well-known figures, including Carter G. Woodson and Dr. Charles R. Drew.

M.T.W. Cruise

Following Brown vs. the Board of Education in 1954, Dunbar's original location was demolished and the school was moved to its current location in Truxton Circle.

As a way of complying with orders to desegregate public schools and avoid a massive shift of students, D.C.'s school officials decided to turn all public schools into neighborhood schools. This had forever altered the make-up of the Dunbar student body and its staff.

With an educational grant and without disturbing the historical integrity of his grandparents' house, Lemuel would turn it into an educational extension of the classroom.

After all, D.C. is the cultural nerve center of the Nation, providing access to such institutions as the Library of Congress, National Archives, National Smithsonian museums, and world embassies. Students would use the home to learn and promote cultural history and diversity.

Each student would spend a semester interviewing their elders and learning genealogy research methodology. Interactive online tools, such as the National Archives, DocsTeach.org, would provide historical documentation to enhance their research. Lemuel firmly believed that one needs to touch, see, hear, and feel history in order to gain a true perspective of it.

M.T.W. Cruise

Students would then present their findings in the form of a Power Point presentation at the end of the semester for a grade and, ideally, college credit.

Lemuel rears back in the old barber chair, soberly aware of the history that resides in the room. The very chair he sat in was an iconic piece of days past. With a smile he glanced at the RCA Victrola that had once belonged to his great-grandmother and the Edison gramophone that had once belonged to his great-grandfather. He had loved to sneak and play with them as a child.

There was the framed, autographed picture of Count Basie and Ella Fitzgerald and tickets to their show at the Carter Baron that his parents attended with his grandfather. They'd had front row seats. His grandfather had fallen asleep during Ella's performance and she had openly teased him about it in her act.

Next to that hung the framed picture of his grandfather shaking the hand of legendary actress and civil rights spokeswoman, Lena Horne, taken during an NAACP convention in New York in the 1960's. His grandfather had vowed, jokingly, never to wash that hand again.

From the "free papers" bearing his ancestors names and physical attributes; the Revolutionary War pension papers; the sign that had hung atop his great-great grandfather's carpentry shop; the newspaper clippings detailing sit-ins and marches; his grandfather's Howard University Dental School diploma; to the reel-to-reel tapes of jazz performances and jam sessions, the house itself was a veritable museum of American history.

EACH ITEM HAD BEEN PAINSTAKINGLY AND METICULOUSLY PRESERVED BY HIS GRANDFATHER. HE HAD BELEIVED IN THE HISTORY IN THINGS; IN PRESERVING BUT NOT RESTORING THEM. HE ALWAYS SAID "THINGS REPRESENTED STORIES" AND THAT IT WAS THE LITTLE INIQUITIES AND BLEMISHES THAT TOLD THE HISTORY OF AN OBJECT AND THE PEOPLE WHO HAD OWNED THEM. THERE WAS **HISTORY IN THINGS** UNTOUCHED.

M.T.W. Cruise

M.T.W. Cruise is a graduate of Hampton
University.

Acknowledgements

Thanks Mom, my editor and sounding board. You are the consummate professional! Thank you for your unwavering support. Thank you for all the unguarded and sincere critiques of my work and for all the suggestions on how to make it better.

Postface

Thank you for taking the time to read *History in Things*. If you enjoyed it, please recommend it to family and friends. As an independent author, word-of-mouth is fundamentally important.

As a child, my grandparents, parents, aunts, and, uncles fostered pride and confidence with stories of our family's history. These stories provided me with the springboard I needed to go forth into the world with pride and perspective.

I still find the utmost enjoyment in listening to my elders' talk of old times and their assorted stories of triumphs, tragedies, and lessons learned.

I believe it is especially important for the African American community to ensure that the next generation go out into the world with a sense of purpose, confidence, and pride.

www.ingramcontent.com/pod-product-compliance
Lightning Source LLC
Chambersburg PA
CBHW050340110726
47899CB00007B/2573